DEATH SCENE

Trish went to the dressing room door and turned the knob. The door wouldn't budge.

"What's going on with—" She stopped talking suddenly as she began to cough. Harsh fumes were beginning to fill the trailer, and Frank and Joe were coughing now, too.

Frank went to the door and pushed it, but nothing happened. He kicked at it beside the knob, but it didn't budge. The heavy gas was quickly flooding the room.

Joe gasped, "We're suffocating!"

Someone had turned the trailer into a huge, comfortably furnished gas chamber!

Books in THE HARDY BOYS CASEFILES® Series

Available from ARCHWAY Paperbacks

THE HARDY BOYS CASEFILES NO. 34

FINAL CUT

FRANKLIN W. DIXON

AN ARCHWAY PAPERBACK
Published by POCKET BOOKS

New York   London   Toronto   Sydney   Tokyo   Singapore

AN ARCHWAY PAPERBACK *Original*

An Archway Paperback published by
POCKET BOOKS, a division of Simon & Schuster Inc.
1230 Avenue of the Americas, New York, NY 10020

Copyright © 1989 by Simon & Schuster Inc.
Cover art copyright © 1989 Brian Kotzky
Produced by Mega-Books of New York, Inc.

ISBN: 0-671-74667-7

First Archway Paperback printing December 1989

10   9   8   7   6   5   4   3

THE HARDY BOYS, AN ARCHWAY PAPERBACK
and colophon are registered trademarks of Simon & Schuster Inc.

THE HARDY BOYS CASEFILES is a trademark
of Simon & Schuster Inc.

Printed in the U.S.A.

IL 7+

Chapter

1

"FRANK. HEY, FRANK! What are you doing? Catching flies?" Joe Hardy whispered.

Joe Hardy had been trying to catch the eye of his older brother, Frank, but caught him in the middle of a huge yawn instead. Both boys were terminally bored by speeches and ceremonies, and right then they were suffering through both. They were standing wedged at the front of a crowd listening to Town Supervisor Gilchrist speak from a raised platform. His amplified voice rang out: "My friends, this is an exciting day for Bayport!"

Joe sighed quietly and slid his silver aviator sunglasses over his blue eyes. Maybe, he figured, he could hide his impatient scowl behind them. When Joe folded his muscular arms across his chest, anyone could see why he was a star football player.

1

Frank's steady girlfriend, beautiful blond Callie Shaw, stood between the brothers and poked Joe with an elbow. "Better play it cool," she warned, gesturing toward the Hardys' aunt Gertrude, who stood next to Frank. She was drinking in every word and staring round-eyed up at the platform of the new WBPT-TV studios.

"I know a new TV studio here in Bayport is a big deal," muttered Joe, keeping his voice low. "But they could be celebrating just as well if I were at the mall. I know we promised to come with Aunt Gertrude, but enough already."

Frank Hardy, a year older and an inch taller than his brother, leaned across Callie and whispered, "Just think of it as survival training. Make a game of it and you won't be so bored."

"Not even that'll work today. There ought to be a law against speeches that last more than ten minutes! They should have a guy with a stopwatch standing on the platform, and when a politician goes over the mark, just drag him off and—"

"Frank! Joe!" Their aunt Gertrude flashed them one of her reproachful glares. "Can't you two keep quiet? Mr. Gilchrist is introducing some famous movie and TV people, and I can't hear with you carrying on!"

"Sorry, Aunt Gertrude," said Frank, raking

back his straight brown hair. "But Mr. Gilchrist does have a way of going on—"

"And on and on," added Joe. "What's more, there's a whole platoon up there ready to take his place. That guy Graham looks like he's got a nice, long, dull speech to lay on us."

"Now, Joe," Gertrude said, wagging a finger at him. "J. F. Graham has done a lot for Bayport."

J. F. Graham was a tall, distinguished-looking, gray-haired man whose face was in the local newspapers at least once a week, usually over a caption that read, "Well-known Financier." For the past twenty years his money had funded shopping centers, housing complexes, and office buildings all over the city. No one had been more important to Bayport's growth than J. F. Graham, who owned or had a controlling interest in a web of interrelated companies.

He stood beside the town supervisor. Behind them were most of the VIPs in town as well as the top dignitaries from the new studio.

Callie nudged Frank. "Is that Jim Addison up there? The actor who always plays really nasty types on TV?"

"I thought I recognized him," Frank replied, nodding.

"Do you remember him in that TV movie, *Murderous Mechanic?*" Callie asked, shuddering slightly.

"He's probably playing the heavy in that movie they just started shooting, *Thieves' Bargain*."

"It's not just a *movie,* Frank!" Gertrude's eyes gleamed with excitement. "It's a *pilot* for a TV series, and they might shoot the whole series right here in town. Maybe even on our street!"

"Sounds like Mr. Gilchrist is winding down, getting ready to finish," Frank noted hopefully.

"Fat chance," Joe replied, shaking his head. "He's just getting his second wind."

Sure enough, the town supervisor glanced down at his notes, and continued as if he had just begun. "At this time I want you to meet the man who will be in charge of the day-to-day operations here at Bayport Studios, an experienced Hollywood veteran and a good friend, I might add—Mr. Mel Clifford!"

A short, deeply tanned man in an off-white suit and open-necked sport shirt stepped forward. He waved, and his sunglasses reflected the glare from the hot sun.

Gilchrist went on at length about Clifford's life and excellent qualities. "And now," he said, "I wish to thank the person who deserves the greatest credit for transforming the old WBPT studios into modern ones—a leading citizen of our fair community and a man whom

I am proud to call a close friend—Mr. J. F. Graham!''

Graham smiled to acknowledge the crowd's applause as the supervisor continued.

"At the conclusion of my remarks, Mr. Graham will say a few words. . . ."

"A few words," Joe whispered, staring over Callie's head at his brother in horror. "My brain's about full right now. Words are going to start leaking out if we don't get out of here—now."

Frank shrugged helplessly. "I'm with you, but Aunt Gertrude looks like she's going to see this thing through to the bitter end. I don't see how we—"

He broke off abruptly when he noticed that Callie had closed her eyes and was swaying back and forth, a hand on her forehead. She looked ill.

"Callie? Are you okay?"

She shook her head weakly. "I don't know . . . I feel kind of sick—if I could just sit down . . ."

Frank said, "Aunt Gertrude, excuse me, but Callie's sick. Would you mind if I took her someplace to sit down and rest?"

"Oh, of course not, dear!" Gertrude gave Callie a concerned look. "You *do* look pale, Callie." She thought for a moment. "Frank, Joe, you two help her find a comfortable place to rest for a while. Don't worry about me, I'll be fine.''

"We'll see you at home," said Joe.

"I'm sorry, Aunt Gertrude," Callie said faintly.

"Don't be silly, dear, you just take care of yourself. Go on, now."

Frank, Joe, and Callie started toward the main gate of the studio, making their way through the crowd. Adding to the congestion were carpenters, electricians, costumers, and painters who were trying to work. The studio was so large that many of the workers had to ride bicycles to get from one place to another.

"Maybe it's the flu," Joe suggested. "There's been a lot of these real weird bugs going around lately."

"No, I don't think so," said Callie, giving Joe a Cheshire cat smile. She was suddenly looking very healthy. "Actually, I think I'm on the road to a complete recovery. I'd probably feel as good as new—"

"With a slice of pizza from the mall!" Frank stared at his girlfriend with respect. "You were faking it!"

Callie looked smug. "Well, we were all desperate to get out of there, and here we are. You can tell your aunt that I just needed to sit down. I'm fine now."

Joe grinned. "Unbelievable! You ought to be an actress. You really looked sick back there."

"I don't think acting is my thing," Callie replied. "Except in emergencies, of course. Did someone say something about pizza?"

Frank laughed. "Okay, okay. You've definitely earned it."

"Pretty impressive setup," said Frank as they walked on. "It's like a little city."

The studio was spread out over a hundred acres. There was a maze of streets and narrow alleys between buildings. The biggest structures were soundstages, where the actual shows were shot. The enormous doors of one stood open so they could glance inside.

"Awesome," said Callie. "You could fit our whole house and yard into just a corner of this thing."

Smaller buildings were identified by signs: Sound Recording Studio, Carpentry Shop, Wardrobe Department.

"There's the gate." Joe pointed to the right. They started past an alley between two sound stages. Suddenly they heard a loud crash, the sound of metal smashing against metal.

"What was that?" Callie yelled.

"It came from down this alley," Joe noted. "Let's check it out." They dashed to the mouth of the alley.

The harsh roar of a powerful engine being revved up filled their ears, and then a pickup truck shot toward them. Callie became rooted to the gound. The truck was going to hit her head-on!

Frank spun and dove for her. The force of his charge carried them back several feet. They hit the ground just as the truck whizzed by. It took a sharp turn and raced for the gate. People scrambled and parted to clear a path for it like the wake on both sides of a ship.

A few angry pedestrians yelled after the disappearing truck as Frank asked Callie, "You okay?"

She laughed weakly. "Now I *really* need a place to sit down."

Joe helped her up and saw how scared she'd been by the near miss.

"That truck had no plates," said Joe.

"Is there anything down there?" asked Frank.

The three peered into the narrow passageway. It looked empty except for a big metal scrap bin piled high with trash at the far end. The truck must have struck the bin initially. They walked down to get a better look.

The bin was full of scraps of wood, paint cans, a broken ladder, and other junk. It looked like an ordinary scrap heap. Except— except for something sticking out that caught Joe's eye.

"Frank," said Joe, "does that look like a foot to you?"

"*Two* feet, actually," said Frank.

"Must be a dummy," Joe decided.

"Probably," replied Frank, "but we better make sure."

The brothers climbed into the Dumpster and began to remove pieces of junk. They worked quickly as more of the dummy came into view. Frank lifted a piece of wood, then suddenly dropped it to jump back.

"What's the matter?" cracked Joe. "Too heavy for you? Let me." He reached down and pulled off the board.

Sitting on the side of the Dumpster, Callie gasped.

"Uh-oh," said Frank.

"That's no dummy," Joe said simply.

Callie said nothing; she only bit her lip and looked away.

The legs were human, and they were attached to a body. The body was dead.

Chapter

2

FRANK AND JOE AND CALLIE had called the police at once. They had given them what little information they had and had been asked to wait.

Since then they had been standing off to one side, apparently forgotten while half the Bayport police department swarmed around the alley. Chief of Police Collig himself was directing the work. Technicians drew sketches, took pictures, measured, and dusted for fingerprints.

Frank finally spotted a friendly face among the ranks of the Bayport P.D.

"Hey, Con! Con Riley!"

Con Riley smiled and walked over to greet the boys and Callie. He was a big, easygoing man, one of the few local police willing to admit that Frank and Joe had helped to solve some tricky cases in the past. To him they were friends, not nuisances.

"Hello there! Trust you to be the ones to trip over a body."

"Yeah, but now no one'll tell us what's going on." Joe frowned and nodded at the busy crime scene.

"What's happening, Con?" Frank asked. "Who was the guy?"

Riley thought for a bit before replying.

"Well—okay. The victim is a writer named Bennett Fairburn. Matter of fact, he wrote the script for 'Thieves' Bargain,' the TV series pilot they're shooting. He was shot by a single thirty-eight-caliber bullet less than two hours before you found the body—about an hour before the speeches began."

"Any leads? Clues?" asked Frank.

Riley smiled, raising his hands. "Whoa, slow down. We just got here an hour ago. Although, as it happens, we *do* have a possible suspect. Some of the television people tell us that Fairburn had some pretty hot arguments with an actor, a Jim Addison. They almost came to blows two days ago."

"Jim Addison!" Callie exclaimed. "He certainly *looks* nasty enough to kill somebody."

"Right, they call him the man you love to hate, I think," Con replied.

"So, what does he say?" Frank asked.

"We haven't reached him yet," said Riley,

"but we will. I wouldn't be surprised to see the whole thing cleared up in time for supper."

"That'd be nice and neat," said Joe.

Frank started to speak, then stopped, looking thoughtful. Then he turned to his brother. "I guess we might as well take off if you don't need us."

"Hang on a second," said Con, and he went over to talk to Chief Collig. After a brief conference, Riley returned.

"The chief says you can go, and that he's grateful for your assistance."

"Sure," said Joe.

"So long, guys," Con said. "Sorry, but I don't think this is one of those whodunits you like so much. Maybe next time."

After dropping Callie off, Frank and Joe headed for home. Frank didn't say a word.

Finally Joe couldn't stand it another second. "Okay, what's on your mind? Spit it out."

"I don't know exactly, but there's something weird about dumping a murder victim where you know there's going to be a big crowd, especially one with lots of media people—TV, newspapers, the works. I can see that the Bayport P.D. wants this thing to have an easy answer, but it just doesn't fit together right."

"Maybe not," agreed Joe, "but it's none of our business anymore."

As they pulled into their driveway, they spot-

ted their dad's car and one they didn't know—
a slick, sporty little foreign job, built for speed
and handling.

"Dad's home," Frank observed, "and it
looks like he's brought company."

Their father, Fenton Hardy, had been a detective with the New York City police department for some years before becoming a private
investigator. He now had an international reputation as a detective.

"Whoever the company is, I like the choice
of wheels," Joe said with an admiring look at
the visitor's car.

"You wouldn't want it," replied Frank. "I
bet it's a real gas guzzler."

Joe turned and gave the low-slung perfor-
mance car one last envious stare.

"I could live with that," he said.

They went in to the sound of their father's
voice calling out, "Frank? Joe? Is that you?"

"It's us, Dad," Frank answered. "We
would've been here earlier but we found—"

"Yes, I know what you found," Fenton cut
him off. "Chief Collig called. Come on into my
office. There's someone I'd like you to meet."

The brothers stopped in surprise just inside
the door. Seated on a couch, across from Fenton, was Jim Addison! He was a big, barrel-
chested man in his late forties, with a face that
could frighten children. Now he only looked
worried. Beside him sat a woman wearing an

elegant silk dress, lots of makeup, and an angry expression. She was talking.

"And I think that it's simply *outrageous* that the police can even *think* of Jim as a murderer! Why, he wouldn't hurt—" She broke off, noticing the newcomers in the room. "Oh. Hello, boys."

Fenton stood up. "Andrea, Jim, I'd like you to meet my sons. The brown-haired one who looks as if he's seen a ghost is Frank. The blond with his mouth hanging open is Joe. Boys, this is—"

"Jim Addison!" they said in chorus.

Addison gave a faint smile. "I hope that means that you're fans," he said.

Fenton gestured to the woman, who was giving the two brothers a dazzling smile. "And this is Andrea Stuart, Mr. Addison's personal manager."

"Delighted, I'm sure," she purred. "My, you two are good-looking! You could break a lot of teenage hearts. Have you ever thought of careers in Hollywood?"

"Uh, no, not really," Frank said. "Nice to meet you, Ms. Stuart."

"Please!" She held up a hand tipped with long, scarlet fingernails. "Call me Andrea."

Fenton spoke. "Frank and Joe assist me in a lot of my work. Do you mind if I fill them in?"

"Go ahead," said Addison.

"We've been talking about my investigating

the murder of Bennett Fairburn. At the moment the Bayport police seem to have only Mr. Addison—"

Addison interrupted. "It's *Jim*."

Fenton went on. "The police think that Jim is their number one suspect."

"Which is ridiculous!" Andrea Stuart burst out. "It's just because everyone thinks that an actor who plays bad guys has to be a bad guy in real life!"

"Actually, there's a little more to their suspicions than that," Frank said. "Con Riley said that the police know of some rather loud arguments between Fairburn and Mr.—er, Jim, here."

"Oh, really?" asked his father. "That true, Jim?"

"Oh, it was nothing," said Andrea. "Just two men blowing off a little steam."

"Jim?" Fenton asked again.

"Well," said the actor, looking uncomfortable, "before I got involved with this pilot, I'd been looking for a chance to play a good guy for a change. I was getting tired of always being the heavy."

"There's a lot more work out there if he can play nice characters sometimes, too," added Andrea Stuart. "It would give his income a nice little boost."

"We agreed to sign onto this deal only because we were told that I'd play a good guy this time," Addison continued. "Also, I was told that if the pilot did make it as a series, I'd be a regular on the show. There was nothing written down about it, but—"

"We just figured we could trust them," finished the manager.

"Then we got the script, and there I was, playing a villain again! A criminal genius, the mastermind of a gang of crooks! And what's more, I was *out* of the regular cast of the series! When I complained, they said they'd work it so I escaped at the end of the pilot, and they could bring me back now and then, but—"

"But *that* means a lot less money," Andrea Stuart chipped in. "Not as many shows, and not as much money per show."

"Well, they had us," said the actor bitterly. "We had signed, and they hadn't done anything illegal. We could have sued them, but it would have cost a ton of money and kept me tied up in court all the time. So we were stuck. And when I found out that the idea to change the script came from Fairburn—well, I guess I got a little angry with him. We did have a few shouting matches—but *murder!* I wouldn't—"

"Oh, *wouldn't* you though?" Gertrude stood in the office doorway, glaring at Addison. "I saw you kill that sweet young girl in *Death at the Drive-in!* And the way you treated your own cousin in *Hot Lead and Cold Blood* was awful!"

"But—but those were just roles, just parts in movies, Miss—Mrs.—"

"This is my sister, Gertrude," said Fenton. "She, uh, sees a *lot* of movies and TV."

"Fenton, I'd be *very* careful if I were you," said Gertrude. "No one can *act* that mean without it rubbing off a little. I don't know—"

"Thanks for the advice, Gertrude," said Fenton, gently moving her out of the office. When she had gone, he turned to Addison and shrugged an apology.

"You see why I'm tired of playing bad guys?" Addison demanded. "This kind of thing always happens! People boo me when I walk into a restaurant, kids run away from me in the street, little old ladies kick me in the shins—"

"And being suspected of murder could cost us a fortune," Andrea added.

Fenton thought a few moments and said, "I think I'm willing to take your case, but first I need you to do something for me."

"Anything. Name it," Jim Addison said eagerly.

"I'd like Frank and Joe to be put to work on the project somehow. To nose around a little."

Jim Addison looked over to his manager, who gave another of her bright smiles.

"I don't think it'll be a problem. They can probably be production assistants—gofers."

Frank said, "As in 'go fer' this and 'go fer' that, right?"

"Right, sweetie," said Andrea. "You'd be little more than errand boys, doing a bit of everything—fetching and carrying, paging actors, whatever.

"Mel Clifford wants to hire as many local people as he can, so if we tell him that a couple of young local students want a job, he should be happy to agree. Especially if we get J. F. Graham to put in a good word for you."

"Would Mr. Graham do that?" asked Joe.

"J.F. will be glad to do me a little favor," Andrea assured him. "He's a pussycat."

Frank and Joe gave each other a quick grin. It was hard to imagine the dignified Graham as a "pussycat," and they doubted that Graham would care much for the label.

"So, Mr. Hardy—Fenton—will you?" Jim Addison leaned forward anxiously.

"You see to getting jobs for Frank and Joe," replied Mr. Hardy, "and I'll take the case. I'll start by getting some background on Fairburn. Frank and Joe, you sniff around and pick up any gossip about him that you can find. Any known enemies, that kind of thing."

"You got it, Dad," Frank assured him.

Jim Addison and Andrea Stuart got up to leave.

"I feel much better knowing that you're on the case," Jim Addison said, shaking Fenton's hand. "And I'll tell you one other thing," he added, looking grim. "Fairburn's friends could fit in a phone booth. You ask around, and you'll see. There are a lot of people who are glad to see him dead, and there are bound to be some who were willing to help him get that way."

Chapter

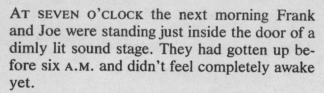

3

AT SEVEN O'CLOCK the next morning Frank
and Joe were standing just inside the door of a
dimly lit sound stage. They had gotten up before six A.M. and didn't feel completely awake
yet.

The soundstage was enormous, like an air-
plane hangar. It was empty except for the far
corner, where a small area was lit from powerful overhead lights. Forty feet above the boys
was a network of narrow catwalks where people walked back and forth, adjusting and setting lights. Dozens of other people were milling
around below, but it wasn't clear what they
were doing.

"So what now?" Joe wondered.

"Look for someone in charge," Frank replied.

"It's seven A.M., and all these people look

20

like they've been here for hours,'' Joe muttered, only half awake. "Don't they believe in sleep in this business?''

Before Frank could answer, a voice called out from somewhere in the vast, dim space. "Hey! You two! Are you Frank and Jim Harley?''

A bearded, balding man in jeans and a shabby sweater came jogging toward them. Static and voices were being emitted from a walkie-talkie on his belt.

"My name's Joe, not Jim, and that's *Hardy,* not Harley, but otherwise you got it right,'' Joe said grouchily.

"Hardy. Yeah, right,'' said the man, making a note on a clipboard. "Right. Okay. I'm Hector Ellerby, the first A.D.—''

"A.D.?'' questioned Frank.

"As in assistant director. I'm the guy you work for. I tell you what to do, and where and when to do it. You have any questions, ask me. You got any problems, come to me. Understood?''

"Well, actually, I *do* have a couple of questions,'' Frank began, but Hector waved him off.

"Not now, I don't have the time. I've got to get over to the office. Trish'll show you around. Trish? *Trish? Trish!* Come on, dear, hustle!''

A soft voice came out of the gloom. "Sorry, Hector, I was just getting—''

"Yeah, right. Look, I have to run. Fred and Jim Hardy, the new P.A.s, are out here waiting. Show them the ropes, will you? Gotta go, bye!"

"That's *Frank* and *Joe*," called Joe, but Hector was already out the door.

"Don't let Hector get to you," said the voice from behind them. "He's all right. A.D.s are always racing around. It's part of the job."

The Hardys turned and came face-to-face with a young woman who, even in the dim light, was obviously very pretty. Her black hair was cut in a short style that perfectly framed her large brown eyes. She wore jeans and a shiny black satin jacket, which said Bayport Studios in electric blue.

"Frank and Joe, right?" She shook their hands. "I'm Trish Cochran. I'm going to direct movies someday. Right now I'm what they call a directing trainee."

"Nice to meet you, Trish," said Frank.

"I'll say," Joe agreed eagerly.

"What's a trainee, exactly?" asked Frank.

"I'm learning all about how movies and TV shows get made. Meanwhile, everybody gets to order me around. Everybody but you, that is. You guys are the only people around here that I outrank. Well, let me show you around. Come on."

Trish led them over to the brightly lit area. There, the Hardys saw that furniture had been laid out, surrounded on three sides by "walls"—large canvas flats anchored by hinged legs and weighted down with sandbags. Through a "window" in one wall Frank and Joe could see a painted backdrop of a city street.

Workers positioned chairs, changed and focused the lens of a huge camera mounted on a wheeled dolly, and maneuvered microphones on the ends of long poles. Others placed props on the desk. Apparently the set was an office of some kind. Two men stood motionless while someone put pieces of tape on the floor at their feet. A crew member measured the distance from the camera lens to the nose of one of the men, who, Trish whispered, were stand-ins.

"What are they standing in?" asked Joe.

"They're standing in for some actors," she explained. "See, they're close enough in size and looks to the actors they work for, so that they can replace them and stand in while the crew focuses the camera and sets up lights and sound. That way the actors don't get tired out just standing around."

Trish walked the brothers over to where a man sat in a canvas director's chair with the name *Ivan* stenciled on the back.

Trish said, "Ivan, meet our new P.A.s Frank and Joe Hardy. Guys, this is Ivan Kandinsky, the director."

Ivan Kandinsky wore a black jumpsuit.

Around his neck hung a viewer, which he would occasionally peer through.

"Frank, Joe. Delighted. Hardy—hmm. Have you, by chance, a relative named Andrew?"

"Uh, no, not that I—" Frank started to say.

"No, no, didn't think so."

A woman ran up with a gun in each hand just then. "Which one should he carry, Ivan?"

"Let's use the forty-five automatic, my dear." Kandinsky turned to Joe, who was staring at him. "Forty-fives have more *presence,* don't you think?"

Joe nodded and Frank tried not to laugh.

They walked over to the camera. There they met Jerry Morrall, the director of photography, a white-haired man with a bushy mustache.

"Welcome to our happy family," said Morrall.

"Nice to be here," replied Joe.

"Sometimes it is," Morrall answered.

"Bizarre," Joe whispered to his brother.

"Over here, guys," called Trish. She stood next to a young man whose hair was almost to his shoulders. He wore wire-rimmed glasses and headphones. In front of him was a rack with a complicated-looking tape recorder and a lot of electronic gear. Frank was fascinated.

"Frank, Joe, this is Teddy Silva, the sound man. Everybody calls him Headcase because he always has those headphones on."

"How you doing?" asked Headcase.

"Say, what kind of a tape recorder is that?" Frank wanted to know. "Looks pretty special."

"It's a Nagra. You find them mostly in studios. Cost about eight thousand dollars."

"Eight *thousand*—" Frank was stunned.

"More or less. Are you into electronics?"

"Definitely," Frank replied.

"Well, hey, let me show you. Trish, think you could hustle me up a cup of coffee?"

"Sure thing. Be right back, guys."

"Mind if I come along with you?" Joe asked, hopefully. He was always more interested in a pretty girl than a tape recorder.

"Sure, come on. You'll need to know where the coffee is anyway. You'll be fetching your share of it. Oh, hi, Vic." A man had wandered up just then. Joe remembered him as one of the stand-ins. He kept walking, looking very sour.

"Oops, Vic's in a bad mood," said Trish.

"He's *always* in a bad mood," noted Headcase.

"That's Vic Ritchey, Jim Addison's stand-in," Trish explained.

"What's his problem?" Joe asked.

Trish explained. "He wants to act, but all he ever does is stand under the hot lights like a statue. Then, when it's time to do the interesting stuff, he's gone. He always doubles for Jim, but he hates it."

"Sounds boring," Frank remarked.

"It's a living," replied Headcase.

"Come on, Joe, let's get the coffee," said Trish. "We have work to do."

They walked over to a food table, on which were a big coffee urn, trays full of doughnuts, rolls, tea bags, sugar, and plastic foam cups. "They go through hundreds of gallons of coffee a day," Trish commented as she got a cup. "And all the sodas and the tea and tons of doughnuts."

"Well, they must burn up lots of energy." Joe handed her a napkin.

"It is hard work, but I love it. I'd almost do it for free." Trish smiled, and Joe stepped back from the urn to give her room to pass. In stepping back, Joe bumped into something very large and solid.

A low voice growled, "Look where you're going, kid! You made me spill my coffee."

Joe turned around and found a squat, powerful man glaring at him. He was wearing a T-shirt, now coffee-stained, over a massive set of muscles. He stared up at Joe from under bushy brows.

Trish quickly said, "Joe Hardy, this is Sam Freed, one of our crew. Joe is a new pro—"

"This stuff is to drink, not to bathe in," rumbled Freed. "You got that straight?"

Joe felt his face getting red. "Sorry," he said. "I didn't mean to—"

"You want to get out of my way so I can get another cup, kid? I'm asking you real nice."

"Come on, Joe," said Trish. "Let's go."

"Yeah, that's a good idea," Freed said with an ugly smile. "Be careful and don't trip over yourself or get stepped on or anything."

Joe was stung by the man's attitude.

"Hey, I said I was sorry. If that's not good enough for you, that's your problem."

Freed stepped closer to Joe until they were only inches apart. "Listen, punk," he said softly. "You better run along, right now, or you're gonna wake up with a bunch of footprints all over your face."

"Try it," Joe answered as he tensed his body for possible action. "You may not find it so easy."

Freed reached out a big hand and grabbed a handful of Joe's shirt.

Chapter
4

ALMOST WITHOUT THINKING, Joe lashed out and broke Freed's hold on his shirt. He braced for the fight that he knew was coming.

A voice called out, "Hey, Freed! You going to take all day? Get back here!"

The big man stepped back and looked at Joe. "See you around—punk," he said softly.

Joe took a deep breath and relaxed. "That'll really make my day," he replied.

As the man walked away, Joe noticed Trish watching him with frightened eyes.

"Sorry," Joe said. "It won't happen again."

It wasn't till midafternoon that Joe had a chance to tell Frank about his run-in with Freed. They'd been on the move all morning—delivering messages, calling actors from their dressing rooms, and bringing food and drink to crew members who were too busy to leave the set. Now they were passing out coffee.

"Freed?" asked Frank. "That guy with muscles? I brought him a soda a while ago, and all he said was 'Thanks, kid.' He was nice enough."

"Well, take it from me," said Joe, "he was ready to punch me out right there."

"Well, you'd just made him spill hot coffee all over himself. Don't make too much of it."

Joe wasn't convinced. "I guess we'll see. You get any interesting information yet?"

Frank shrugged. "No time to make small talk with anyone. I've been kept running."

Joe said, "I enjoy investigations, but being a waiter is a drag."

"Come on, the camera crew wants coffee, too," a voice said from close by.

Jerry Morrall had just worked out a camera angle and chosen the lens for the next scene. Now he was sitting in his chair, watching his assistants make the necessary adjustments. Frank handed him a cup of coffee.

"Thanks, Frank. So, how do you like show business so far?" asked the director of photography.

"Oh, it's okay. Interesting people."

Morrall chuckled. "Interesting, huh? I like your choice of words. Yes, they're interesting, all right."

Before Frank could ask Morrall what he

meant, Joe came up and asked, "Who's the big guy sitting against the wall over there? He hasn't moved all day." Joe pointed to a large, round man who sat with his chair tilted against the wall, wearing a cowboy hat down over his eyes.

"Oh, that's Alvin," said Morrall. "He's the unit's driver. But his *real* specialty is sitting. You'll never find a better sitter than Alvin. He can sit there for hours on end."

"Does he ever do any driving?" Joe asked.

"Sure, now and then," said Morrall. "But not while we're shooting here."

"Did you know that guy who got killed, the writer?" asked Frank.

"Fairburn? Sure, I knew him." Morrall looked at Frank suspiciously. "Why?"

"Oh, no special reason," Frank said quickly. "Just curious. Somebody must have had it in for him, I guess," he added, trying to lead the conversation.

Morrall leaned back with his coffee. Frank could almost see him struggle with his love of gossip and his fear of talking too much. Soon, though, the urge to gossip won out.

"Well, guys, just between us, there were a *few* people here who weren't sad to see the last of Bennett Fairburn. Take Mel Clifford."

"The one who runs the studio?" Joe said.

"Uh-huh." Morrall nodded, leaned forward again, and lowered his voice. "He used to be a hotshot Hollywood movie producer once upon a time. Then he got himself into a mess. Seems he wrote a few checks and signed somebody else's name. The guy who blew the whistle on him was Fairburn. That was the end of Mel in the movies, and he figured it was Fairburn's fault that he works in TV now. So when they ran into each other here, well—"

"Jerry!" called one of his assistants. "We're ready to shoot."

"Okay," Morrall said, rising from his chair. "Hector, anytime now."

"Let's lose the stand-ins," Ellerby ordered. "Bring in the A team! Ready, Mr. Kandinsky!"

The stand-ins left, and the actors came in. The set was the office of the private eye and hero, played by tall, handsome Preston Lawrence. Monica Malone, a beautiful brunette actress, played his girlfriend. Lawrence was made up to have a bruised and swollen eye, and a bloody bandage was pasted on his forehead.

"His bandage needs blood," said Kandinsky.

"Makeup!" shouted Ellerby. "More blood on Mr. Lawrence's bandage!"

A man ran in and carefully applied some fake blood from a bottle with a Q-tip.

"Okay, now let's rehearse it once. Something the matter, Monica?'' said the director. Monica Malone was pouting angrily.

"Ivan, I *told* you and *told* you, if the camera's *here* and I'm *there* on camera right, you get my *bad* side. Why can't I be by the desk, and Preston over there where I've been standing?''

Now Preston Lawrence looked mad. "Oh, come on, Monica! If we switch places, then no one can see my black eye and bandage! I got beat up in the last scene, remember?''

Watching this exchange, Frank poked Joe with an elbow and winked. Joe stifled a laugh.

"Now, now, let's be pals,'' urged Kandinsky, jumping between his actors. "Monica darling, we *have* to do it this way, dear, or it won't match up with the other shots, you understand? But then we'll turn the camera *around* and shoot your *close-ups* with your *good* profile—not that you don't look gorgeous from *both* sides, dear—and it'll be *fine*. Trust me on this, okay?''

"Well—oh, all right,'' the actress said, giving Lawrence one last dirty look.

"Fantastic!'' exclaimed Kandinsky, walking back to his chair and wiping his face with a handkerchief.

"Give me a break!'' Joe whispered to Frank.

Frank nodded. "I wish Callie could see this.''

With the crisis solved, the master, or the full scene, was quickly shot. Then the crew got ready for the close-ups, which meant turning the camera around, changing some lights, and moving furniture. The actors, who had seemed to be very much in love only seconds before, walked away from each other without a word. The "B team"—the stand-ins—took over.

Just then Mel Clifford came bustling onto the set and called out, "Jerry! Over here!" With Clifford was a tall, very thin man in a dark suit. Morrall joined them and the three moved away to talk in private. Frank and Joe, watching curiously, noticed that Morrall looked worried. The tall, skinny man left then, almost running.

Headcase called over to the Hardys, "Guys, come over here a sec, will you?"

They went over to the sound man's equipment. "Just stand there and sort of block me from everyone," he said. "Great, stay right there." Frank and Joe were in front of Headcase, and out of the corner of his eye Joe saw him take out a long microphone set in a plastic reflector, like a small dish antenna, and aim it at the secret powwow.

"Headcase, what *is* that thing? What are you doing?" asked Joe.

"Don't look at me," Headcase whispered back. "This is a shotgun mike with a parabolic reflector. It'll pick up a whisper fifty feet away if it's aimed right— Ah, got it!"

Frank was amazed. "You mean you're listening in on—"

"Shhh! Not now, Frank, I'm concentrating. Well, look who's here!" Headcase said.

The thin man had returned, bringing J. F. Graham with him.

After a few minutes of careful listening, Headcase announced to Frank and Joe, "We have a problem here. The film from yesterday's shooting went to a local lab for processing, and they've ruined it. That's a day's work blown— bad news on our schedule. They've decided to air-express all the film from now on to a lab in Los Angeles—at least until they know what went wrong here. Okay, guys, you can relax."

Frank stared at the long-haired sound man. "Do you listen in on private conversations often?"

Headcase looked offended. "Hey, what's the big deal? I mean, I'm not blackmailing people or anything! I just like to keep track of what's going on."

"What if you get caught?" asked Joe.

Headcase grinned. "So far I haven't been."

"But if you did?" persisted Joe.

Headcase shrugged. "With my skills, I'd have no trouble finding another line of work."

"What other kind of work?" Frank wondered.

"Oh, I'm pretty good at putting together all kinds of electronic goodies," said Headcase.

Joe shook his head. "Well, it's your business, I guess."

"Frank! Joe! Can we see you, please?"

Jerry Morrall was signaling them to join him, Mel Cifford, J. F. Graham, and the thin man.

"These are our new production assistants, gentlemen," Morrall said. "Frank and Joe Hardy. Boys, this is Mel Clifford, who runs Bayport Studios, and this is Mr. J. F. Graham, who recommended that you be given jobs here."

Graham smiled. "You're both interested in television production?"

"Yes, sir," Frank replied.

"Getting more interested every minute," said Joe.

"Splendid!" Graham said. He nodded to the thin man, who nodded back and left quietly. "I think these two young men are just the ones to help us with our problem."

"Us? How can we help?" Frank asked.

Jerry Morrall answered. "All the film we shoot today has to be rushed to the airport to be flown air-express to L.A. You guys know your way around here, right?"

Graham cleared his throat and said, 'I'd better be running along. Nice to meet you, boys." Then he was gone.

The brothers looked over at Alvin, still leaning back in his chair. "What about him?" Joe wanted to know. "Isn't this his kind of job?"

"Alvin?" Morrall said. "Oh, no, we have to keep him here in case one of the actors needs to be driven back to the hotel. Well, can you handle this? We'll send Trish along to look after the film itself."

Joe's face brightened. "It'll be a snap. Right, Frank?"

"Like he says," Frank agreed, "no problem."

Shooting ended a few hours later, and the Hardys met Trish at the stage door, carrying a big stack of film cans.

"Can I give you a hand with that?" Joe said. He took the cans from her, getting a grateful smile from the girl.

"How far is it to the airport?" asked Trish, jogging to keep up with the boys.

Frank shrugged. "Maybe twenty-five miles."

"That plane leaves in forty-five minutes," said Trish. "Can we make it?"

"No sweat," Frank assured her, opening the side door to their van, a black beauty with a powerful customized engine. Soon they were on a hilly road, which wrapped itself ribbonlike around some tight curves as it rose and fell.

"Is this the fastest way to the airport? Why not the highway?" Trish asked from the backseat as Frank whipped the van into a hairpin turn.

"This time of day, we'd get stuck in rush-hour traffic," answered Joe from the seat next to her. "This way, it'll be clear sailing all— Whoa! Sorry." As the van cornered, he slid against Trish, his seat belt stretching its full length. A second later he slid in the *other* direction, against the door. The film cans clattered beside him, sliding from side to side.

"There's no need to floor it, not on *this* road. Take it easy," Joe said, bracing himself in his seat.

Frank stared at the road, then at the speedometer, knuckles white as he gripped the wheel.

"This joyride isn't *my* idea! Grab something—we've lost our brakes!"

The van skidded through a left turn, and there, headed straight up the hill at them and filling more than its half of the road, was a huge flatbed truck!

Chapter

5

THE TRUCK LOOKED ENORMOUS, lumbering toward them like a modern-day dinosaur. Its air horn hooting angrily was almost drowned out by a scream from Trish behind. Frank struggled to stay cool as he wrestled with the wheel, the clutch, and the gearshift to edge as far as he could to the side of the road. A dense growth of trees left little maneuvering room there though.

The van was on the dirt shoulder, and tree branches whipped at the windows as it sped by. A heavy branch smashed the right sideview mirror just as the flatbed was on top of them, filling the windshield with its chrome grille.

The Hardys and Trish braced for the crash, but it never came. Horn still blaring, the truck screamed past, an inch separating it from the van. But Frank had no time to relax; he slammed the shift down into second gear and heard the engine howl in protest. It worked. The van slowed a little, just enough to keep them from flying off the road on the next outside curve. Suddenly the downgrade ended, the road began to climb, and the van slowed even more.

"Everyone all right back there?" shouted Frank, throat dry and heart pounding.

"We're okay, I think," his brother yelled. "How about stopping this thing?"

"I think I see a place up ahead—brace yourselves!"

To the right of the road was an old turnoff, long abandoned. It ended in a few feet in a thick tangle of undergrowth. Frank dropped into first gear and slowly let out the clutch. The engine screamed as he aimed for the bushes. There was a last screech of tires, a bone-jarring thump, and they stopped with branches scratching at their doors. There was complete silence for a few seconds.

"Trish? Joe? How you doing?" Frank finally asked, rubbing a tender spot where his ribs had hit the steering wheel.

"All in one piece, I think," said Joe shakily. "Trish?"

"I—I— Wait till my heart slows down a little! Frank, if you were trying to impress me with your driving skills, you could have found an easier way!"

Frank took a deep breath and got out to join Joe in checking out the damage. After a quick inspection, Joe shook his head. "This van isn't going anywhere for a while, except behind a tow truck. The left front end is crumpled in against the wheel and the right side looks like it's been through a war."

He surveyed the area. There was no sign of anyone—no houses, no lights twinkling in the early twilight.

Headlights shone around a curve and caught them in the glare, blinding them for a second. They hardly saw the car that pulled up to a stop.

"What happened? Do you need help?" asked the driver, leaning out his window to take in the crumpled van and its dazed passengers.

"We had an accident—lost our brakes," Frank replied. "But we're okay. If you could just give us a lift to a phone so we can call a tow, we'd appreciate it."

"Sure," the man said. "There's a little diner not too far away. Hop in."

"I'll go," said Joe. "I'll call a garage in town."

"Call Hector Ellerby, too," added Trish. "He has to know we missed that plane."

"And call a taxi," Frank said.

Joe turned back to Frank halfway to

the car. "You think this has anything to do with—"

Frank cut his brother off. "Later, Joe. When we're alone. Right?"

Frank looked at Trish, who was wearing a puzzled expression, obviously trying to figure out what Joe had been going to say. She kept quiet and didn't ask any questions, though.

Sometime later the battered van had been hauled away, and Frank, Joe, and Trish were dropped off in front of the Hardy house. "Come on in for a minute, Trish," suggested Frank, "and then we'll get you back to the hotel—or wherever you want to go."

"Joe said Ellerby wanted me to drop this film at the studio," she replied. "They have to figure out how to get it to L.A. tonight."

"We'll take you in just a minute," said Joe, and the three entered to find Fenton Hardy waiting.

"Dad, this is Trish Cochran, she works on the film. She was with us when we had a—"

"Little accident," Frank finished. "Trish, this is our father, Fenton Hardy."

"Nice to meet you, Trish," said Fenton. "Is everyone all right?"

"We're fine, Mr. Hardy," Trish answered.

"That's good. Trish, will you excuse us for a minute?" Fenton led his sons into the kitchen.

"What happened?" he asked.

"There was no fluid in the van's brake cylinder," replied Frank.

"Was it an accident?" Fenton said.

Frank thought, then shrugged. "There's no evidence one way or the other."

Fenton nodded and then turned to Joe. "Does Trish know about the case?"

"We haven't said a word to her," Joe said, assuring his father. "But she couldn't be involved."

"Why not?" Frank asked. "Come on, Joe! I mean, sure she's pretty, but—"

Joe's face turned red. "That's not what I mean! All right, say someone wanted us out of the way and messed with our brakes. She was right there with us. If we'd been taken out, she'd have been killed, too!"

"As it stands, we can't be absolutely certain that she's an innocent bystander, so we have to keep her out of this for now," Fenton said. "Now, what else have you got?"

Frank and Joe quickly filled their father in on what they'd learned, especially from Jerry Morrall. Joe told them about his run-in with Sam Freed.

"What does this Freed do?" asked Fenton.

"He's a gaffer," replied Joe. "He moves scenery, furniture—heavy stuff like that."

Frank said, "He didn't seem all that bad to me. He did get steamed at Joe, but don't forget, he'd just spilled hot coffee on himself."

"Just steer clear of him—if possible," advised his father.

"I'm willing if *he* is," Joe replied.

"I've been checking Fairburn's past," said Fenton. "He worked as a police-beat reporter for years in Boston. I've phoned a detective I know there, and he's sending me a rundown on the man, plus copies of his big stories. Oh, I'll arrange for a rental car for as long as your van is in the shop, and tonight you can use my car to take Trish where she needs to go."

"I have a date with Callie," Frank said.

"I guess that leaves me," said Joe, trying not to sound too eager.

The three Hardys rejoined Trish, who was curled up on the couch leafing through a magazine.

"Sorry we took so long," said Frank.

"That's okay," she said. "I needed a little time to get myself together anyway."

"I can give you a lift to the studio now," said Joe, grinning at her.

In the car Joe tried to make small talk with Trish, but it seemed she had no interest in anything but television and movies.

After they handed the film to Ellerby, he got rid of them instantly.

"Thanks, kid, gotta get this film on a charter plane we have standing by. Then I gotta see about extras for tomorrow."

When they pulled up at the corner near the

front of the hotel, Joe said to Trish, "If you feel like something to eat, we could—"

Trish smiled but shook her head. "Can't tonight. I'll just grab something. The editor's going to let me watch while he does some cutting. Isn't that great?"

"Yeah, wonderful," Joe replied. He hopped out of the car and walked her to the hotel and said good night.

Joe strolled unhappily back to his father's car and wondered if there was anything other than television that interested Trish. He had his hand on the car door when he felt a steely grip on his shoulder.

"Nice to run into you again. What do you say we finish our little talk?" a gravelly voice said in his ear.

Before Joe could move, another hand shot out and grabbed his arm, twisting it painfully behind his back. Joe tried to wrestle free, but he felt a stab of pain in his shoulder as his arm was wrenched even harder.

"Keep fighting, kid, and I'll break it off."

Then the goon shoved Joe ahead of him into a dark alley just around the corner.

Chapter

6

THE ALLEY WAS a deep U shape, bordered on three sides by the rear walls of the hotel. Joe felt himself being shoved forward and didn't stop until he was smashed up against a brick wall. He tried to clear his head, but things were happening too fast. He heard faint traffic noise, too far away. His arm ached, and his face burned where it had been scraped against the bricks.

He turned slowly to face his attacker. Freed! Joe knew one thing—he didn't want to fight him right then. He needed to try to get on the man's good side if he was going to be able to stay at the studio and gather information. "I'd forget about that girl if I was you, punk," Freed growled. "Matter of fact, I'd forget about the TV business altogether. I think you ought to take an early retirement—real early.

Like, just don't show up tomorrow morning. It ain't your line of work, you know?''

Joe resisted the impulse to rub his shoulder or check the blood that he could feel warm on his face. He tried to think. Was Freed bullying him just for the fun of it? Or was he delivering a message?

Joe moved a step away from the wall. "What's the problem anyway?" he demanded. "What's it to you whether I work there or not? I don't get it."

Freed folded his arms across his massive chest. He looked hard and mean in the dim light. Shadows cut deep hollows in his face. "Listen, junior, I don't have to give you explanations. I don't like your face, and I don't want you around no more. How's that for a reason?"

Joe grinned at the man. "You sure know how to hurt a guy's feelings. And here I was, hoping we could be buddies and all."

Freed took a deep breath. "Okay, little man, I guess you don't listen too good. Maybe when I mess up that pretty face of yours, you'll get the message and wise up."

Joe measured Freed with his eyes. The gaffer was shorter than Joe, but he was solid— about Joe's weight. Joe just hoped he was quicker.

Freed took a few shuffling steps toward Joe,

who circled warily, keeping his distance. He wanted Freed to make the first move.

"This'll be *fun*," Freed purred, and swung up a roundhouse right that started from the hip. Joe dodged, and Freed connected with nothing but air, which threw him off balance.

Joe countered with a straight left that caught Freed square on the nose, drawing a geyser of blood. Joe stepped back, trying to keep some distance between them.

Freed blinked, lowered his head, and bulled forward, windmilling his thick arms in a hail of hooking punches aimed at Joe's ribs. Joe back-pedaled and landed another left—this time on Freed's ear.

One of Freed's wild punches caught Joe just then in the side. It was only a glancing blow, but it hurt enough to make Joe realize that if the man ever connected with Joe with full force, it would be all over.

They swapped a few more punches, and suddenly Freed changed tactics. He lunged straight at Joe, ducking a left that Joe threw, and grabbed Joe around the waist. He locked his hands together and began to squeeze. Joe tried to work free, but Freed was too strong.

Trapped in the bear hug, Joe couldn't breathe. He had to break loose fast. Freed grunted, and lifted Joe off the ground while maintaining the crushing pressure.

Desperately Joe grabbed a double fistful of

Freed's hair and yanked hard. The gaffer let out a bellow, and his hold eased off long enough for Joe to squirm free.

Gasping, Joe danced back a couple of steps, and Freed charged after him. He threw a wild roundhouse right, and Joe dropped his head. The punch flew over his shoulder and smashed against the wall. Freed roared in anger and pain.

When the stocky gaffer rushed forward again, Joe slipped to the side, and Freed flew straight into the wall. For an instant Freed was stunned, unable to keep his guard up. Joe landed first a short left hook to the midsection, and then a right uppercut to Freed's jaw. The gaffer's knees turned to rubber, and he sank slowly to the ground.

As the man was struggling to get up, Joe bolted and ran for the car. He wanted to consult with Frank. He also wanted to put some mileage between himself and this gorilla.

But as he opened the car door, he heard Freed's voice from the alley. "Where do you think you're going, punk? We're not done yet!"

Quickly Joe started the car and put it in gear. As he drove by the mouth of the alley, Freed lunged forward and almost grabbed hold of the door. Joe sped away, watching the powerful form grow small in his rearview mirror. Good thing he didn't grab that door, he thought to himself, or he'd probably have torn it off.

Later that evening, when Frank came home from his date, he eyed the scrapes on his brother's face and whistled.

"Did you and Trish have a little disagreement?" Frank asked, not cracking a smile.

Joe shook his head. "Trish had a heavy date to watch film being edited. That girl has a one-track mind, so I dropped her at the hotel. Then, as I was leaving, Sam Freed grabbed me. He's the one I had the disagreement with."

Frank looked thoughtful. "It looks like you're still in one piece. How did *he* look?"

Joe said, "I was lucky. I slowed him down long enough to get away. It would take a lot to stop him. Funny thing, though"—Joe rubbed his arm and winced—"I can't figure out if Freed was just going after me on his own, or if maybe he was told to scare me off."

Frank replied, "I don't know. Maybe he's still sore about the coffee. Maybe he's interested in Trish himself and doesn't want you hanging around her. Seems like he just took a serious dislike to you."

Joe felt his ribs to see if he had suffered any injury. "I don't know why. I'm such a nice, friendly guy." Joe frowned. "Seriously, though, the coffee business was just an accident. It wasn't enough to start a war over."

"You planning on telling anyone about what happened tonight?" Frank asked.

"No way," exclaimed Joe. "Let it ride. We don't want the police all over the studio, making everybody uptight. No one'd ever talk to us."

"Right you are," agreed Frank. "Maybe tomorrow, we—"

The doorbell rang, cutting him off, and almost instantly it rang again.

"Pretty late for callers," Joe said.

"Maybe it's your buddy Freed." Frank winked at his brother.

As the Hardys went to the front door, the doorbell rang a third time, a long, insistent ring. Frank opened the door, and Andrea Stuart swept in and began to pace back and forth like a tiger in a cage.

"They'll never get away with it!" she said angrily. "We'll sue that department for every last cent!"

"Won't you come in," Frank asked dryly.

"Where's your father?" demanded the manager. "I have to see him. Now."

"Why? What's so important?" Joe asked.

She glared at him.

"I'll get him right away," Frank assured her. "Meanwhile, please sit down."

She ignored Frank and continued pacing.

Frank and Fenton appeared a moment later.

"What is it, Andrea?" asked the detective.

"Your brilliant local police just arrested Jim. He's down at headquarters now. I'll have that chief's badge for this! I'll have the best lawyers in the country here in the morning, and we'll sue the city for . . . defamation of character and false arrest and—"

"All right, Andrea, settle down," Fenton said quietly. "Let's have the facts. They arrested Jim? For murder?"

"Of course for murder! Those stupid, bumbling—"

"Something new must have come up," said Joe. "They wouldn't just arrest him for no reason."

Andrea wheeled around and nailed Joe with a long, hard look. But Fenton spoke first.

"There's no point in standing around here. Let's go downtown and find out exactly what is going on. Frank? Joe? Coming?"

"Right with you," replied Frank.

They reached the main police building shortly before midnight and asked to see whoever was in charge of the Fairburn murder. A minute later Chief Collig strode into the room.

"Good evening, Mr. Hardy."

"Chief, I didn't expect to see you down here at this hour."

"When we break a major case, it always gets my personal attention. You're here about developments in the Fairburn matter?'' He barely nodded to Frank and Joe. They knew that he considered their interest in past police investigations to be unnecessary and sometimes obstructive.

"Mr. Addison has hired me to look into it," answered Fenton, "and I've been going on the assumption that he is innocent. The fact that he hired me gives some weight to my presumption."

"Yes, I could see that it might appear that way," said Collig. "But it looks like you backed the wrong horse this time, Mr. Hardy. He'll be formally charged in the morning."

"This is—of all the thick-headed—how dare you even think such a thing?" Andrea Stuart sputtered.

Chief Collig looked at her coldly. "And *you* are—"

"This is Andrea Stuart, Jim Addison's personal manager," Frank said.

"How do you do?" said Collig. "We make arrests only if we're very sure of ourselves."

"On what grounds, Chief?" asked Fenton. "I assume you've got hard evidence."

Collig nodded, trying not to show his pleasure in having solved the case so quickly. "Earlier this evening we turned up an eyewitness who saw a very nasty argument between Mr. Fairburn and Mr. Addison—"

Andrea Stuart erupted again. "Why, that's

ridiculous! Who is this—this—eyewitness anyway?"

But Chief Collig shook his head. "We don't reveal the names of witnesses, ma'am."

"Some jealous stagehand, I'm sure," she said, pacing again. "Of course Jim and Fairburn argued. But that's no reason to charge Jim with murder. You're just trying to get publicity using Jim because he's a star."

Collig's face turned pale. "I've got a solid case here. I don't care about publicity, and you'd better watch yourself."

Frank tried to catch her eye. "Andrea, you're not helping your—"

But she wasn't listening. "Our lawyers will be here in the morning," she said, glaring at Chief Collig. "And you'll be lucky to still wear a badge once we've finished with you and your two-bit department."

Collig's lips were pressed together in a thin line. "It's a very good idea to have a lawyer here," he said to Andrea. "Make it a good *criminal* lawyer. Because our witness—not a stagehand, by the way, but a respected citizen of Bayport—heard Addison and Fairburn arguing only *two hours* before the body was found."

"But—"

"He was only twenty yards away, and recognized them both," Collig went on. "What's more, he heard Addison say that Fairburn had a bullet coming to him, and that he'd be pleased to deliver it personally. We got the right man, Ms. Stuart. As far as I'm concerned, this case is airtight. Jim Addison murdered Bennett Fairburn.''

Chapter

7

IF THE WITNESS STOOD UP, the case against Addison looked pretty solid. Fenton Hardy had a short private conversation with the chief and came out of his office shaking his head.

"I tried to get Collig to release Jim to me," he said. "I argued that Jim wouldn't run because it would amount to an admission of guilt and because he's too well-known to stay hidden for long. Collig wouldn't buy it."

Andrea Stuart's jaw was clenched. "I'm calling J. F. Graham right now to *demand* that he use his influence to get Jim out of there."

"Even Graham might not be able to do much," Frank said.

"We'll see about that!" she snapped. "Where's a phone?"

"There's a pay phone through that doorway," Joe replied, "but—" He stopped. She was gone.

She returned wearing a satisfied grin. "J. F. is on his way here right now," she said.

"In that case, we'd better go," said Frank.

"Go?" she asked. "Why?"

"He shouldn't see us here," replied Joe. "As far as he knows, we're just a couple of kids with an interest in TV production."

The Hardys were back home and Frank and Joe ready for bed when the doorbell rang. Frank opened the door and admitted a tired, pale Jim Addison, along with Andrea Stuart, J. F. Graham, and the tall, thin man who always seemed to stick close to Graham.

"Jim, are you all right?" asked Fenton.

"I guess so," the actor answered. "But being locked up gets to you. J.F., here, told the chief he'd vouch for my sticking around."

Graham stepped forward. "Mr. Hardy, I want to tell you how pleased I am that you're working for Jim. Oh, this is my private secretary, Norris. Norris, this is Fenton Hardy, the detective, and his sons, Frank and Joe, who are helping their father out on the case."

Norris nodded to them. Though they were angry at realizing that their security had been broken, Frank and Joe kept their silence.

"Well, Mr. Graham—" Fenton began when his sister, Gertrude, appeared in the hallway.

"I heard the doorbell and the talking. Is there anything wrong? Oh, Mr. Addison! What's happened? You look just awful!"

Addison replied, "I'm fine, Gertrude, really. Just tired, that's all."

Gertrude blushed and said, "I'm sorry about the other day. I get carried away sometimes. But I know just the thing to fix you up—a nice steaming cup of cocoa. Let me just—"

"No, really, you needn't go to any—"

"Now, it's no trouble at all," insisted Gertrude, heading for the kitchen.

Andrea Stuart said, "Mr. Hardy, have you learned anything important about Fairburn's past? You said you would check on it."

Fenton replied, "I don't think we need to keep Mr. Graham and Norris any longer."

"Oh, come on, Mr. Hardy," Andrea urged. "We can trust Mr. Graham. He *is* on our side."

But Graham spoke up. "Ms. Stuart, I think it's best for me to leave. Mr. Hardy is quite right to keep things private. If there's anything more I can do, just ask."

The financier and his secretary departed, and the others went to Fenton's office.

"I think you were very rude to Mr. Graham," said Andrea Stuart. "After all he's done for us—"

"How come Graham knows all about us working for you?" asked Joe.

Andrea gave him a cold stare. "I *beg* your

pardon. Are you trying to tell me my business?"

Frank said, "It's *our* business when our cover is blown. You weren't supposed to talk about us to anybody without clearing it first."

The manager turned to Fenton. "Mr. Hardy, really. Are my dealings subject to approval by your *children?* This is ridiculous."

"Children!" Joe was furious.

Fenton gave Andrea a cold look. "Frank and Joe are absolutely right to be worried, Mrs. Stuart. The more people who know about our job, the harder it becomes, and the more dangerous as well."

"Dangerous? Oh, please!" Andrea sneered. "Let's skip the cheap melodrama. How could I persuade Mr. Graham to get your boys hired, or to get Jim out of that cell, without telling him what's going on here?"

"Melodrama, huh?" Joe said. "Well, we had a little joy ride today on a mountain road with no brakes. That wasn't melodrama, that was real life." He related the story of the van ride.

Addison was shocked. "But you're okay? You weren't hurt?"

"We were lucky," replied Joe, "and Frank is a really great driver, or you'd have needed two new gofers tomorrow."

Andrea Stuart, however, waved it off. "You don't mean to suggest that J. F. Graham goes around fiddling with brakes, do you? He isn't a hoodlum, he's a respectable businessman. It must have been an accident.''

"Andrea.'' Fenton leaned forward and fixed her with a steely look. "Let's get this clear. You are not to talk to him or to anyone else about this case. Do we understand each other?''

"Oh, all right, if you insist. Now, what have you learned about Fairburn?''

Fairburn's past as a crime reporter suggested nothing to either Jim or Andrea.

"What about this eyewitness?'' asked Frank. "Got any ideas about that?''

Addison shook his head.

Fenton said, "Jim, when I saw Chief Collig, he showed me the transcript of the eyewitness's story. I can't reveal his name, but I know the man and he's an honest citizen, with no stake in this business. He says he heard you tell Fairburn that he'd earned a bullet and now he was going to get it. We have a problem here. Can you explain it at all?''

Jim slammed his hand on the arm of his chair. "Explain it! No, it's completely crazy! I was in my hotel room, alone, until just before that opening ceremony, studying my script. I never *saw* Fairburn that day! Of course, I have no way to prove it. If you don't believe me . . .''

"You know—maybe something could be— arranged,'' Andrea said.

"Arranged? Meaning what?" Joe asked.

Gertrude bustled in, carrying a tray. "Here's some nice cocoa for everyone, and some home-baked cookies. Now, Mr. Addison—"

"Just Jim, please, Gertrude," said the actor.

"*Jim,* then. A cup of cocoa will make you feel much better. I'll just leave you all to your business." Gertrude quickly left the office.

"What did you mean, something could be arranged?" Frank said.

Andrea shrugged. "If we found witnesses who would swear that at the time of the murder Jim was, oh, let's say, having breakfast with them miles away, why, they'd *have* to clear him."

Joe frowned. "But Jim was alone, in his room at the time."

Andrea waved it off. "*You* know that, sweetie, and *I* know it, but we can still get witnesses—for a price."

Abruptly Fenton stood up. "That's foolish talk, Andrea. And I have to tell you that if you ever try such a thing, not only would we drop the case, but we would have to go to the police and tell them about this conversation."

Now Andrea got up and glared at Fenton. "If you cared more about helping your clients and less about little legal formalities—"

"Andrea!" Jim Addison's voice rang out. "That's enough! It's late, and we're all tired. Let's go and let the Hardys do their job. *Now.*"

Andrea blinked and looked confused for a moment. "Yes, of course. You're right, Jim. I apologize if I— I'm sorry."

The visitors got up to go, and Jim Addison noticed the untouched cocoa.

"Thank Gertrude for her hospitality," he said to Frank with a grin. "Good night."

Fenton Hardy showed them to the door and rejoined his sons in his office.

Frank shook his head. "That Andrea Stuart is something else."

"Can you believe her trying to get us to go along with phony witnesses?" exclaimed Joe. "She could be real trouble."

Frank sat up straight. "Maybe she's mixed up with this murder herself! With her attitude toward the law—maybe she set Jim up—"

"How could she have set up the argument that witness overheard?" Joe asked. "Maybe the lady *is* bent, I don't know. But right now I'm more worried about who else she told about why we're really at the studio. Even if she's honest, she's dangerous."

"I think we should turn in and worry about it in the morning," replied Frank, yawning. "We're going to be short of sleep as it is, and tomorrow, we've got to—"

Crash!

The sound of smashing glass shattered the nighttime silence.

"That came from the living room!" Frank shouted, charging out the office door.

An engine was gunned, and someone took off at high speed.

Frank reached the living room first, and stopped short just before his father and brother joined him. Daggerlike shards of glass from the living room window lay scattered all over the carpet. In the middle of the room lay a brick, a piece of paper wrapped around it. Joe picked his way carefully through the mess to get at the brick. He carried it back to where all three of them could read the message scrawled in block letters on the paper.

"Mind your own business. Next time we'll use a bomb."

Chapter

8

THE NEXT MORNING Frank and Joe were back at work on the sound stage. Sam Freed was there, too, but he hadn't reacted at all when he saw Joe. No one had any comments about the scrapes on Joe's face either.

The Hardys had decided not to let anyone, including the police, know about the brick and the bomb threat. "If we don't keep quiet about it," Frank had said, "we won't be able to do our job because the police will be following us around to protect us."

"It sounds like a bluff anyway," Joe said. "If someone goes after us with a bomb, it's like saying that the case against Jim isn't open-and-shut after all."

While a shot was being prepared, Frank and Joe were learning about wireless microphones from Headcase.

"See, you can hide the mike on a costume, like behind a button," Headcase explained, holding up the tiny gadget, "and then the actor puts this transmitter in his pocket. I pick the sound up on this receiver. It's great, say, when the actors are in a car, and you can't use a boom mike or run wires."

"Frank, Joe!" Trish came over. "Mr. Addison needs you in his dressing room."

Jim Addison's dressing room, unlike the boxy little trailers that the minor actors had, was large and comfortably furnished. It was set some distance from the stage, isolated from the noise and bustle, with only a few equipment trucks around it.

The Hardys found J. F. Graham and Norris in the trailer there along with Addison and Andrea Stuart. Drawn curtains over the windows and the air conditioning made the room dim and cool. A stereo played softly in the background.

"Come in, boys," said Graham, smiling. "I have some information for you. I had Norris check to see if anyone working on 'Thieves Bargain' might have a criminal record. He's made an interesting discovery. Tell them, Norris."

The secretary, who wore either the same or an identical black suit, opened a folder. Then he read aloud in a thin, reedy voice: "Freed, Sam. Arrested five times on assault charges, convicted twice. Served eight months in prison after the second conviction. Released three times for lack of proof.''

"Why, the man is a gangster! Why not just have him fired?'' Andrea Stuart blurted out.

"Not without definite evidence that he's committed a crime,'' Graham said. "The union wouldn't stand for it, and a man is innocent until proven guilty. We don't have any evidence against him, do we?''

Frank and Joe exchanged glances but said nothing.

"Then,'' Graham went on, "let's simply keep an eye on this fellow. He might be—''

There was a knock on the door, and Mel Clifford burst in. "Hello, J.F., I wasn't told you were going to be here today. What's this meeting all about? Or shouldn't I know?''

"Take it easy, Mel,'' said Addison.

"If I'm not wanted . . .'' Mel said sulkily.

"Oh, that's all right, honey.'' Andrea Stuart hooked her arm through his. "We just want to see that Jim isn't tangled up with this horrible murder more than necessary, that's all.''

Mel nodded, and then looked suspiciously at Frank and Joe. "And what about these kids?''

"They've been helping—'' Andrea started to explain, but Addison cut in sharply.

"Andrea! Stop!''

Mel's eyes jumped from person to person in the room. "Oh, so there *are* some secrets, are there? What's happening? You hatching a plan to give the cops some suspect besides Jim? I mean, he's still the prime suspect, right? And with reason, right?"

"If the cops wanted another suspect," said the actor, glaring at Clifford, "they wouldn't have to look very far. Would they, Mel? You figure that Fairburn ruined your Hollywood movie career, right? Can *you* account for your whereabouts on the morning of the murder?"

"Me! Why, you big, overrated ham! We all saw you practically strangle Fairburn when—"

The two men stood up, Addison towering over Clifford. He said, "Remember, Mel, *you* have the criminal record, not me! *You're* the forger!"

Mel Clifford's face went from tan to bright red. "That's it! One more word, and I'll—"

J. F. Graham stepped between the two. "Cut it out, both of you! We have enough problems on our hands without this kind of nonsense. Mel, come with me, and cool down. Excuse us, please."

Graham and Norris left, taking the furious Mel Clifford wth them.

Once they had left, Joe spun around to face Andrea Stuart. "You just won't learn, will you? You were going to tell Clifford about us a minute ago! Why don't you buy an ad in the local papers? Then you wouldn't have to spend all your time telling everyone in person."

"I've known Mel for years!" she exclaimed. "He's a pussycat! He couldn't be involved—"

"That's not the point," Frank said. "My dad told you not to tell anyone why we're here. You might tip off the murderer that—"

A knock on the door stopped Frank. Trish poked her head in.

"Mr. Addison, you're needed on the set."

Addison took a deep breath. "Thanks. Andrea, come with me."

"Jim, is it all right if we use the phone in here?" asked Joe.

"Feel free," the actor answered. He and his manager left, along with Trish.

"Who are you going to call?" Frank asked.

"I want to tell Dad about Andrea Stuart and her big mouth before she really messes us up."

"Good idea," Frank replied.

As Joe picked up the phone there was another knock at the door. Frank opened it, and there was Trish again.

"Guys, how come you're not on the set? They're going to be looking for you."

"We have to call the garage," Frank said quickly. "About the van. It won't take long."

Joe put the phone down. "Couldn't get through," he explained to Frank. "Trish, if you have a minute, we'd like to ask you about something. Come on in, it won't take long."

"Well, okay, but this better be quick." As she stepped into the trailer she examined the scrapes on Joe's face. "What happened to you?"

"I had a little accident last night," said Joe quickly. "Tripped and fell in the driveway."

"Yeah, Joe's always tripping over his feet or something"—Frank smiled—"but we put up with him anyway."

Trish didn't look convinced.

"Frank and I have been wondering about this guy who got killed," said Joe.

"Fairburn?" asked Trish.

"Right," said Frank. "We heard Jerry Morrall talking about how Fairburn and Mel Clifford didn't get along, and then Mel and Jim Addison almost had a fight going in here—"

Trish grinned. "Jerry Morrall told you that, huh? *He* should talk!"

"What do you mean?" asked Frank.

Trish obviously enjoyed a little gossip, too. She leaned forward and lowered her voice. "Everyone on this project knows that Jerry and Fairburn hated each other's guts for years."

"How come?" asked Joe.

"They went to court once over who had the rights to a story they both wanted to film, and Fairburn won. He always teased Jerry about it to get him steamed up."

"That's one bit of information that Jerry

would never have told us about himself,"
Frank said.

"This Fairburn sounds like a real sweet
guy," Frank observed.

Trish shrugged. "I didn't really know him,
but everyone says he was a creep. He had a
nasty sense of humor and always knew how to
get at people, knew just how to needle them
and drive them crazy."

Joe looked at Frank thoughtfully. "Sounds
like people would've stood in line for a chance
to murder him."

Trish gave the brothers a suspicious look.
"Why are you so interested in Fairburn any-
way? I thought you were here to learn about
TV production?"

"Oh, yeah, we are," Frank assured her.
"But a murder is pretty exciting stuff, you
know. We just figured you'd know some of the
inside dope, since you've been working here,
around all these people, that's all."

Trish stood up. "Well, we should really be
back to work. This isn't the time to be—"

A nearby truck started up with a roar and
drowned out her voice. Trish went to the door
and turned the knob.

The door wouldn't budge.

She pushed harder, but it remained firmly
shut. She turned to look at the Hardys.

"What's going on with—" She stopped talking suddenly as she began to cough. Harsh

fumes were beginning to fill the trailer, and Frank and Joe were coughing now, too.

Joe pulled back the curtains covering the windows, but instead of a view there was an expanse of wood that completely sealed off the view—and any chance of ventilation.

"Someone's boarded over the windows!" Frank snapped, his voice breaking into coughing spasms. The fumes grew heavier.

Frank went to the door and pushed it, but nothing happened. He kicked at it beside the knob, but it didn't budge. The heavy gas was quickly flooding the room.

Joe gasped. "We're suffocating!"

The trailer had been turned into a comfortably furnished gas chamber!

Chapter

9

"HELP! SOMEBODY, HELP US!" screamed Trish, and then she lapsed into a fit of helpless coughing.

"No one'll hear," gasped Joe.

Frank saw Trish panting for breath. "Lie down flat, the air's better near the floor," he said hoarsely.

Joe grabbed a chair and smashed at the window. The glass shattered, but the boards remained in place. "No good," he wheezed.

Frank saw that Trish, lying on the floor, was barely conscious. His lungs ached as he labored for enough oxygen to keep him conscious. "Not much time," he said faintly. "Try the phone!"

Joe staggered over and picked up the receiver, then dropped it. "Line's dead. Must've been cut."

Desperate, Frank looked around. Suddenly he looked up and saw, in the roof of the trailer, a small plastic skylight. It was too high for him to reach without help.

He dragged a small coffee table directly under the skylight and picked up a heavy brass Emmy statuette from a shelf. Jumping on the table, Frank hammered as hard as he could with his oxygen-starved muscles. With his second blow he cracked it and with the next he smashed his way through.

"Joe! Get Trish up here and I'll pull her out!" Frank hoisted himself up and onto the roof. Reaching back, he took hold of Trish's semiconscious body and dragged her up beside him. Joe quickly followed, and all three sat there silently, inhaling lungfuls of fresh air.

After a few minutes the three dropped lightly to the ground. They examined the windows, which had been covered by half-inch-thick plywood. The wood had been held in place by the heavy-duty silvery adhesive tape used on TV and film sets by gaffers and referred to as "gaffer tape."

"No wonder you couldn't knock that wood loose from inside," Trish said to Joe. "That tape is made to hold heavy stuff in place."

Joe looked at the trailer door. A wooden wedge had been stuck between the door and the frame. The harder they shoved and kicked, the firmer the wedge had gotten lodged in place.

Frank had led the way around the trailer. Now he called to the others, "Come here and check this out."

A length of hose had been run from the exhaust of one of the huge tractor rigs that the studio used for hauling equipment into a vent in the wall of the trailer. Both ends of the hose had been held in place with the same silvery tape that had secured the plywood.

"Someone sure worked fast to get this set up," Joe said. "Or maybe it was more than one person."

"It would almost have to have been more than one," Frank responded. "It was done fast and silently."

"All right, you two!" Trish stood facing the brothers, and her eyes were angry as well as frightened. "I want to know what's going on here! Last night when we lost our brakes, you told me it was an accident. I suppose this was an accident, too!"

Joe focused over her head. "We aren't supposed to—"

"Hey, don't tell me that!" Trish yelled. "I could've died last night, and I could've died just now! You owe me the truth!"

Joe's eyes darted to Frank, who shrugged a reply. Then they focused on Trish once again.

"You're right," he said to her. "We couldn't

be sure before, but after this—I'm going to tell her," he said to Frank. "If Dad asks why, it was my idea."

"Go ahead." Frank nodded. "I agree."

Quickly Joe outlined to Trish why they had come to work on "Thieves' Bargain." As she listened, Trish's anger gave way to fascination.

"So whoever killed Fairburn may be trying to get to you before you can find out the truth," she said. "Is that it?"

"It's a good bet," answered Frank. "Who knew we were in that trailer just now?"

Joe counted them off. "Graham, Norris, Addison, Stuart, and Mel Clifford. Anybody else?"

"No," answered Frank, "unless—Trish, when you were looking for us to tell us to go see Addison in his trailer, did you ask around much before you spotted us? Who did you talk to?"

The girl thought back, and then nodded. "I checked several places before I saw you— Oh, I see, you're right. I stopped by the camera crew, I talked to people in props, wardrobe . . . And every time I left word that you should be told to come to Jim's dressing room."

"So, just about anybody on the set *could* have known that we'd be there," Joe concluded.

"Maybe someone on the set might have seen someone coming from here," suggested Frank.

The three went toward the door of the sound stage.

As they approached the door, Joe said, "There's Jim now! Maybe he saw someone. Hey, Mr. Addison! Jim!"

The figure turned and looked at them curiously as they got nearer. It wasn't Addison but his stand-in, Vic Ritchey, taking a breather. Red lights flashed around the door, indicating that shooting was going on inside, and that no one could enter or exit until the lights went off. Sitting near Ritchey was Alvin, with his hat pulled down over his eyes, in his usual director's chair leaning against the wall.

"Uh, hi, Mr. Ritchey," said Joe. "Is Mr. Addison working in there?"

The stand-in nodded glumly. "Yeah, he's in there getting his face on film while I cool my heels out here. Business as usual."

"Mr. Ritchey, did you notice anyone coming from the direction of Jim's trailer in the last ten minutes or so?" asked Frank.

"No, not since Addison did," replied Ritchey. "Of course, I was inside until they sent for him."

"How about you, Alvin?" asked Joe.

There was no response.

"Alvin?" repeated Joe

There was a slight movement from the body in the chair.

"Hello?" came a sleepy voice from under the cowboy hat.

"Did you happen to see anyone coming or going from Mr. Addison's dressing room?" asked Trish.

Alvin slowly lifted a hand to the brim of his hat and raised it so that he could see who was talking to him.

"Sure did," he said, lowering the hat brim again.

"Who?" asked Joe excitedly.

There was a long pause.

"Who what?" asked Alvin.

Frank took over. "Alvin, who did you see around Mr. Addison's trailer? It's kind of important."

The hat brim was nudged up again, and Alvin looked calmly at Frank before replying.

"Lots of folks. There are always lots of people running every which way around here. Don't know what they're in such a hurry about, racing around like they do. I never pay them much mind myself." Down came the hat brim.

"Great," observed Joe sarcastically.

The flashing red lights went off, and the stage door opened. The first one to appear was Hector Ellerby.

"Oh, good. Here you are," he said, leafing through a stack of papers on his clipboard. "Tomorrow is a big day, guys. We're shooting

76

this humongous gun battle at the end of the picture, okay? We'll be on location downtown, and you're going to help with traffic control. Here's a map of where we'll be. Be there by seven A.M. sharp. Got that? Hey, how come you two are hanging around outside anyway? We've been working *inside*."

"Actually—" Joe began, but Hector stopped him with a hand gesture.

"Sorry, guys, I'd love to stand and chat for a while, but I have to check out the locations for tomorrow and make sure we've got the cars arranged and rigged, and I've got to make a sketch of the location for Mr. Kandinsky. See you."

And off he jogged.

The door opened again and out came Addison and Stuart. Frank caught the actor's arm.

"Something's come up. Can we see you over by your trailer?"

As they walked Addison back to his dressing room, Frank and Joe and Trish explained about their near miss with death. Addison looked grave, and even Stuart, for once, didn't make fun of what had happened.

"Who do you think could have done it?" Jim asked when the brothers had finished their story.

"We don't know yet," Joe answered. "But one thing is for sure. *Somebody* around here definitely knows why we're working on this project and wants to make certain we're stopped." He cast a quick glance at Stuart, and she looked away.

They rounded a corner and started up toward the trailer. Frank said, "I can't figure how they got that plywood over the windows. They didn't have enough time . . ."

"*I* had those windows boarded up by the crew," said Addison. "I take naps in there and I wanted to block out the sunlight and the noise."

As they came up to the dressing room door, Addison said, "I don't like it. I don't want anyone getting hurt for my sake. It's getting too dangerous for— *Hey!*"

A stocky figure had popped out from around the corner of the trailer and blundered straight into Addison. His arms were loaded with gaffer's tape and lengths of hose. It was Sam Freed.

Freed threw the hose and tape in Addison's face and took off surprisingly fast, with Frank, Joe, and Trish on his heels. Freed did have a ten-yard lead, which Frank quickly whittled down to two. But before Frank could bring him down, Freed sidestepped a stagehand pedaling a studio bicycle and threw the man and bike down in the boys' path. By the time they had disentangled themselves, Freed was racing toward the crowded main street of the lot.

"He'll probably head for the front gate. We

can't lose him in the city," Frank said as he and Joe sprinted in pursuit, Trish close behind.

They reached the main street and looked around. Joe tapped Frank's shoulder. "There he is!" Following Joe's finger, Frank saw the gaffer turn a corner and run down a narrow alley between two large buildings.

"What's down there?" asked Joe as they dashed that way.

"We'll see in a second," Frank replied as they dodged the traffic to reach the alley. It dead-ended and was empty.

Each of the buildings bordering the alley had a door, and the brothers tried both. They were locked. Trish caught up to them just then.

"Freed's vanished," Joe told her. "He ducked in here, but now he's gone."

Trish said, "The building on the left is the scene shop, where they build the sets. I'll bet Freed has a key to that door."

"Come on!" snapped Frank, and he and Joe raced around to the front of the buiding. The enormous sliding doors in front were fully open. Frank poked Joe in the arm.

"He's over there!" he shouted.

A group of carpenters and painters had just left the building, and Freed was walking with them. He appeared to be trying to blend in so that he could make his way to the main gate. But he whirled around at Frank's shout and spotted the Hardys.

He broke into a run, scattering people like bowling pins, and ducked around the corner of a huge soundstage. Frank and Joe followed him just in time to see a side door of the stage close. Trish came panting up beside them.

"He went in there," said Frank. They opened the door and peered inside.

It seemed empty and very dim. Only a few bare bulbs set high up near the ceiling gave any light. The enormous space was silent, eerie. Quietly they steppped all the way in, easing the door closed behind them. They stood motionless, listening hard, but heard nothing.

"He's got to be in here somewhere," Frank said, "but we'll never find him in the dark."

"There's a switch box over by the front doors." Trish's voice echoed three times in the empty space. "I can light up the whole place." She started toward the switch box, which was on another wall.

As Joe stood rooted to his spot, waiting for more light, he heard a creaking and then a metallic clink from somewhere high above him. Looking up, he watched spellbound as a huge object started falling through the gloom. Trish was right under it!

Chapter

10

JOE DOVE FORWARD and tackled Trish just as something large and heavy hit the concrete floor with an explosion of glass and metal that sent thousands of tiny shards whirling.

"Cover your faces." Joe spoke into his arm, and his voice was muffled.

A powerful floodlight lay a few feet from them. It would have crushed anyone standing under it.

Now they heard mocking laughter overhead.

"He's up on the catwalks!" yelled Joe, brushing off the bits of glass that clung to his arms.

Frank called back, "I'm going up after him!"

Joe turned to Trish. "How do you feel?"

She took a shaky breath, but her eyes were steady when she looked at him. "If you hadn't shoved me, I'd be . . . I would have . . ."

She couldn't bring herself to finish.

"For what it's worth," said Joe, "I think Freed probably thought it was Frank or me under him."

Trish shook her head. "I have to stop hanging around with you guys. But I'm okay, I think. Let me get those lights on."

A moment later the entire building was brightly lit. Joe saw Frank halfway up a metal ladder bolted to the wall. Directly above him at the top of the ladder stood Freed. He had a long wrench ready to throw.

"Frank! Above you!" shouted Joe.

As Freed flung the heavy tool, Frank swung out and away from the ladder, pivoting on one hand. The wrench dropped past him and clattered to the floor.

The catwalks were made of wooden planks, about four feet across, set on steel frames. They were arranged in a grid covering the whole floorspace of the soundstage, so that lights could be hung and focused on any spot below.

As Frank reached the top of the ladder, Joe was scrambling up to join him. Meanwhile, Freed ran along a catwalk, away from the Hardys.

"We have him cornered!" Joe said.

"Wrong!" snapped Frank, pointing across to the opposite corner, where another ladder was bolted to the wall. "Let's box him in. I'll cut across, and you chase him down."

The brothers raced in different directions. Joe's speed made him a dangerous receiver of deep passes during football season. Now he closed on Freed, who was alarmed to see Joe on his heels. Realizing he wouldn't be able to reach the ladder before Joe caught him, he turned onto one of the catwalks that led out over the middle of the floor.

But the Hardys were faster and in better shape. Frank quickly shifted to cut the gaffer off, and Joe raced after him in pursuit. Seconds later Freed found himself standing, his back against the catwalk's guardrail, with Frank on one side and Joe on the other.

Freed turned toward Joe and feigned a move in that direction, freezing Joe momentarily. Then he whipped around and ran full speed at Frank, ramming him hard with a shoulder. Frank was knocked against the rail, out of breath, and Freed tried to get by toward the ladder, but Frank dove and just caught Freed by the ankle, sending the thug sprawling on the planks.

Both were quickly on their feet, facing each other. Frank lashed out with a right cross. He hit Freed high on the cheekbone, backing him up a step. But Freed closed with him. He placed a foot behind Frank's ankle and tripped him up. Frank landed hard on the catwalk.

Instantly Freed was on Frank, shoving at him and rolling him. He was going to push him off the planks and down to the concrete forty feet below! Frank felt himself sliding toward the edge with nothing to grab on to.

But Joe came in behind Freed and got in a kick behind the knee. Freed's leg buckled and he lost his balance. Frank scrambled away.

Just as Joe was about to lunge forward, Freed pulled out a long and deadly-looking switchblade knife. Both brothers had to retreat just out of Freed's reach. He turned from Frank to Joe, stabbing out with the gleaming blade. Suddenly Joe darted forward, making the thug lunge. Joe then dove low for Freed's legs while at the same instant Frank hit him chest-high from the other side.

The knife went pinwheeling into the air, and Freed hit the deck with Frank on top of him. Cursing under his breath, Freed bucked Frank off and lunged at Joe, who had regained his feet.

"Not this time, Sam," Joe said, stepping out of reach and driving his knee up and into Freed's jaw. The thug collapsed and lay still.

Panting, the brothers grinned at each other. "The coach would be proud of us," said Frank.

"I *knew* all those scrimmages would come in handy someday," Joe replied. Then he yelled down, "Trish! Find a phone and call the police."

That evening after dinner Frank and Joe sat with their father in his office. They leafed through photocopies of Fairburn's old newspaper stories.

Before settling down to this chore, the three had exchanged their information. The brothers had told Fenton about their day, ending with the Bayport police hauling off Sam Freed.

"The fact that someone wants us out of the way seems to put Jim Addison in the clear," Frank observed. "That's what we told Chief Collig."

"But he said that there was nothing to tie Freed to Fairburn's murder," Joe added. "So he was treating it as a separate incident."

"Well," said Frank thoughtfully, "he may have a point. I mean, we've turned up a lot of people who hated Fairburn, but there's no history that we can find between him and Freed."

"What did you hear about Fairburn's past from your buddy in Boston?" asked Joe.

Fenton pulled a piece of paper out of an envelope. "You can read this over later if you like, but here's the gist of it: Fairburn had a reputation back then as a heavy gambler who was always in debt, always borrowing from the other reporters. He was too friendly with some of the criminals that he wrote about, in the opinion of the other police-beat writers.''

''Not exactly a model citizen,'' said Joe.

The three Hardys continued to look through the file of stories. Suddenly Joe stopped and said, ''Take a look at these.'' He gave his brother a handful of clippings.

Frank checked them over. ''They're about a gang that pulled off a string of big heists twenty-five years ago,'' he said to Fenton. ''Apparently when they broke up the gang, they never caught the brains of the outfit. The stories identified him only as 'Gallagher.' ''

Frank tossed the copies on the desk. ''These stories read just like the plot of 'Thieves' Bargain,' '' he said. *''Exactly* like it. There's no way it can be a coincidence.''

Joe added, ''And this Gallagher is just like Jim Addison's character. The mastermind.''

Fenton picked up the stories. ''Well, I suppose it figures that an ex-crime reporter would turn to his own old material for a TV script,'' he said.

''Yeah,'' said Frank, ''but Jim said that when he was first told about the TV pilot, it was completely different from this. Then, when Jim got the script, he saw that Fairburn had changed it. Why?''

Joe shrugged. ''Maybe he just thought it was a better story than the other one.''

Frank shook his head. ''You don't rewrite a

script completely just before shooting. It wasn't just a little bit here and there, it was a total rewrite, and that—''

The phone rang and Fenton answered.

''Hello? . . . Oh, hello, Con . . . Yes. *What?* . . . When? . . . I'm going to put you on the speakerphone so you can tell Frank and Joe yourself. Just a moment.''

Fenton put down the receiver and punched a button. ''It's Con Riley. Okay, Con, go ahead.''

The policeman's voice sounded strained. ''Hi, Frank, Joe. I've got some bad news for you.''

''What's up, Con?'' asked Frank.

''Sam Freed was being taken for mug shots and fingerprints, and I don't know how it happened, but he somehow managed to overpower his guards and get away. We haven't been able to find him.''

''When was this?'' asked Joe.

''A half hour ago,'' Con replied. ''We've got an all-points bulletin out on him, and we're combing the city. I figured you ought to know.''

Frank's lips were pressed into a thin line. ''Well, thanks for the word, Con,'' he said. ''You'll be sure to keep us posted, right?''

''You can count on it,'' said the tinny voice over the speaker. ''And, Frank? Joe? Stay on your toes. This guy is one mean customer. He really has it in for you two. He put two cops in the hospital, and the last thing they heard him say was that he was going to kill those two Hardy brothers!''

Chapter

11

AFTER CON RILEY'S CALL, Frank and Joe waited for their father's reaction. He said, "I guess I don't have to tell you two to watch yourselves until this guy is found."

"We'll be careful," Frank assured him. "But we still have a job to do."

"Right," agreed Joe. "Anyway, tomorrow we'll be working in a huge crowd all day. Freed isn't going to pop up there. I mean, he may be a hood, but he isn't crazy."

The next day the crew and cast were set up in downtown Bayport, on a block that had been cleared of traffic for the day. Freed was nowhere around.

"Nobody seems to miss him much," said Joe.

"A nice, friendly guy like that?" cracked Frank. "I can't imagine why."

The scene being shot was a gun battle between the gang and the police. At the end of the battle the gang would be captured, except for the character played by Jim Addison, who'd escape.

Frank and Joe had walkie-talkies. They were stationed on a sidewalk just off camera. They had to keep any passersby or curious onlookers from wandering into a shot. Hector Ellerby had actually spent a whole minute with them giving them instructions.

"Remember, guys, this kind of scene, with a lot of extras and guns and stunts and cars and fightings, costs a bundle of money. And if we have to reshoot any of it because some civilian gets in front of the camera, then it'll cost *two* bundles. "So watch the walkers and gawkers, and don't fall asleep, okay? I'm counting on you guys."

"We'll stay awake," Frank replied.

"You can trust us," said Joe.

There had been no further word from the Bayport police about Sam Freed. He was still at large. But neither of the Hardys was especially worried about his showing up on location.

"Maybe he's left town," Joe suggested hopefully but not really believing it.

Before any actual shooting, there were several rehearsals. Police cars raced up, cops spilled out, and heavy gunfire erupted between cops and robbers.

Everything had to be organized to the last detail among a hundred performers, three cameras in various locations, and all the other crews.

During breaks between rehearsals, Frank and Joe met the special-effects wizard, Max. He was a leathery older man in a baseball cap and sat at a big electronic console, where he could set off the small charges that looked like bullets striking targets by remote control.

The Hardys listened as Headcase explained how the actors were supposed to be "shot." They had very light explosive charges taped to their bodies, which were protected by thin protective shields. In some cases, in close-ups, there would also be plastic bags of stage blood designed to burst when the actor was "hit." Other charges had been fastened to walls, to look like bullets smashing into the walls when they were set off by the man at the console.

The special-effects wizard would control all this. But everything had to be carefully planned and gone over again and again, to reduce the possibility of expensive retakes. Ideally scenes like this were shot only once.

Frank and Joe found it all as interesting as did the "civilians," what the crew called everyone not involved in their line of work.

They watched everything from just out of camera range, on the nearby sidewalks.

"Where's Jim Addison?" Joe asked Jerry Morrall at one point.

"Oh, he's not here yet. On a long shot like this, where you can't really see his face, Vic Ritchey can do just as well. Better, maybe."

"How come?" Joe wondered.

Morrall gave one of his ironic smiles. "Well, Ritchey is younger and a little more athletic than Addison, so Addison generally lets Vic do the running around whenever he can. Ritchey really can look amazingly like Jim. Also, it's pretty dull and time-consuming, so Jim would just as soon sit it out." Morrall winked at Joe. "You know what they say, rank has its privileges. First we shoot the whole scene from a distance. What we call the 'master.' And then we start working on reverse angles, point-of-view shots, and close-ups—*then* Jim'll go to work."

After still more rehearsal, Addison *did* appear, hopping out of a limo and vanishing into his dressing room trailer. During a break the brothers went to see him and told the actor about Fairburn's old newspaper stories.

"What do you make of it, Jim?" Frank asked. "Does it give you any ideas?"

Addison shook his head—it meant nothing to him. He was too concerned about the scene he had to do to think about anything else.

"Could one of you stick around and go over my lines with me? I'd sure appreciate it."

Just at that moment the Hardys' walkie-talkies crackled, and Trish's voice sounded.

"Frank, Joe, we're about to shoot. Better get to your stations."

"Roger, we copy," said Joe into his mouthpiece. "Sorry, Jim, but we have to hold back the crowds of your admiring fans."

"*My* fans, huh?" Addison grinned. "Not very likely. But I'll bet you that there's a whole regiment of Preston Lawrence fans there. That's what you get when you play he-men and heroes."

On location Ivan Kandinsky gave his star last-minute instructions. Lawrence listened intently, nodding every few seconds. Then he got into a car and drove off out of camera range.

Kandinsky gave the thumbs-up signal to Hector Ellerby, who had picked up a bullhorn.

"Can I have your attention, everyone? We're about to shoot a very tricky scene, so I want you all to be alert. You people watching over there, please help us out. We're happy to let you watch, but you have to keep *absolutely silent* while we're doing this and stay where you are. If we have to retake this master shot, it'll be hours before we can get it all ready to go again. Thank you for your cooperation." He put down the bullhorn and picked up his walkie-talkie.

"Cameras ready? Sound? Special effects?" One by one, he checked in with each department and got an okay. Then he picked up the bullhorn.

"Drivers, start the cars! Wait for my signal to move! Lights!"

A battery of floodlights turned what was a bright day even brighter.

"Camera!"

Three cameras began to roll.

"Slate the scene!"

Three assistant camera people ran in front of their cameras carrying slates with the scene number chalked on them and hinged sticks, called clappers, on top. Each assistant held his slate in front of the lens, read off the scene number, clapped the clappers, then ran out of camera range.

"And—*action!* Go ahead, drivers!" yelled Ellerby.

Half a dozen squad cars came screaming around the corner into the shot, sirens wailing and red lights flashing, and squealed to a stop. Twenty-five actors and extras in police uniforms piled out of the cars and spread out behind them. A window in the building they were facing was shattered, and a gunshot was fired from inside. Then a burst of gunfire crackled as the "cops" and the actors playing the gang, holed up in a building nearby, blazed away at one another with blanks. One bad guy yelped, clutched his chest, and fell halfway out a window.

Preston Lawrence gave orders and gestured with his hands. Some of the actor/police started charging the building. There was a louder burst of gunfire. Another villain was hit, screamed, and fell all the way out of a window, landing on a thin pad below that was carefully placed just out of camera range. One of the policemen grabbed his shoulder, and fake blood dripped from between his fingers.

Frank and Joe watched the crowd from their stations with one eye but followed the scene with fascination. Joe thought that it went like some kind of super-complex football play, brilliantly run. Frank thought of a really involved chess game.

Since it was obvious that the spectators weren't trying to get too close to the action, the brothers gave more and more of their attention to the action before the cameras.

Joe was so caught up in what he was seeing, he hardly noticed when one shot sounded different from the others. It was sharper, a little louder. Then a chip of the stone from a wall near his head flew off with a whining noise.

Joe looked around but saw nothing unusual. He picked up his walkie-talkie and whispered into it, "Frank. Frank. Do you read me?"

Frank was a few yards away, and whispered

into his own transmitter, "I read you, Joe, what's—"

Suddenly another loud shot hit home above his head. Before he could duck, a bit of stonework flew, scratching Frank's cheek. He put a hand to his face, and it came away with a smear of blood on it.

He said urgently to his brother, "Joe, take cover right now. Someone's using the noise of the fake gunfire to snipe at us, and he isn't using blanks!"

Chapter

12

WHILE HUNDREDS OF UNLOOKERS gasped at the fake gunfire and staged fighting, Frank and Joe were caught up in a real fight for their lives.

Joe dove for cover behind a parked car as a bullet smashed the wall right where his head had been a second before. The crowd gasped and pointed but didn't know what was happening only a few feet away. It was just as well, thought Frank, who had knelt behind the shelter of another car. Otherwise the situation could all too easily turn into a general panic.

Joe put his walkie-talkie close to his mouth. "Can you figure out where the sniper's shooting from?" he whispered.

Frank had been scanning the area. "He has to be up on one of the roofs across the street, whoever it is."

Now Joe, also looking from one roof to the

next, saw a flash of movement from the one directly across from their sidewalk position. The barrel of a gun suddenly appeared, and somebody's arms and head. But at that distance and angle it was impossible to tell who it was.

"Frank," Joe said softly into his mouthpiece, "did you see the gun?"

"Affirmative," replied Frank. "He seemed to pop up to take another shot, and then realized that we had gone to ground. He knew he didn't have a clear line of fire."

"Let's take him as soon as the scene is done," Joe said, and Frank agreed.

The scene ended, and Kandinsky yelled, "Cut! And print!" as the crowd began to applaud.

The Hardys leapt from their cover and sprinted across the street. Reaching the door of the building where they'd seen the sniper, they ducked inside. The roof was four stories up, and they took the stairs two at a time. At the top of the last flight of steps was the door to the roof. It was standing slightly ajar.

They paused and, with great care, slowly pushed the metal door open. They leapt back as a burst of automatic fire greeted them.

"Looks like we found the right place," said Frank as they crouched behind the door. "Did you see the shooter?" Joe asked.

"Yeah," replied Frank. "It's Sam Freed."

"Looks like he *is* crazy after all," said Joe. "How do we handle this?"

"How about if one of us distracts him while the other one jumps him?" suggested Frank.

"Great idea!" Joe snapped. "Let's see, he's got an Uzi or something and we have zip. How do we distract him, with funny stories?"

"The building alongside this one is a story higher," Frank said. "You stay here. Give me exactly one minute and then slam that door open with a lot of noise. I'll come at him from behind, off that taller roof."

Joe replied, "You have to run down four flights of steps here, and then *up* five flights next door. Let's make it ninety seconds. You're not as young as you used to be."

"And you're not as funny as you think you are," responded Frank. "Okay, ninety seconds. Check your watch, starting—now!"

Frank started down the stairs, and Joe remained in a crouch by the door, keeping his eyes focused on his watch's second hand.

As Frank reached the street, he heard Trish call out to him but didn't answer as he ran into the neighboring building.

He pounded up the five flights and rushed onto the adjoining roof. He moved quietly to the edge and looked over. Freed was squatting with his back to Frank behind a large metal ventilator hood, cradling an Uzi.

As the ninety seconds ended, Joe kicked the

metal door open. It swung around and crashed into the wall. He yelled, "Here we come, Freed! Ready or not!" Then he jumped back out of the line of fire. Freed swung his Uzi and fired a burst. The bullets kicked up tar and gravel from the surface of the roof, while others smacked into the stairwell wall, barely missing Joe.

As Joe moved, Frank swung over the edge and dropped the single story down to the other building. Freed was focused on the open doorway. Abruptly he sensed someone was behind him, but before he could turn and fire, Frank hit him with a shoulder in the small of the back. The thug was knocked forward, sprawling to the ground.

"Joe!" shouted Frank. "Move it!"

Joe broke from his cover and charged Freed, whose Uzi lay just beyond his outstretched arm. Freed gave the younger Hardy a murderous look and launched himself forward. He grabbed the gun, pointed it at Joe, and squeezed the trigger.

There was a dry click. Either the clip was empty or the gun had jammed.

Frank reached down to grab him from behind, but with surprising quickness Freed whirled around. He reversed the gun and lashed out at Frank with the grip. Frank ducked, but the blow caught him on the shoulder with numbing force, and Freed kicked clear.

Joe was on him instantly. But he hit Freed high, and the tough gunman dropped lower and arched his powerful back, bucking Joe up and over him. Joe hit the roof and vaulted, disappearing from sight.

The Hardys picked themselves up and took off after Freed. The roof Freed had dropped to was one story lower. They were landing on it as Freed raced for the door to the building's stairs.

Before the Hardys could reach the door, Freed had darted through it and slammed it behind him. Joe tried it, but it wouldn't budge.

"He's jammed it or locked it!" Joe shouted, banging the metal in frustration.

They could hear footsteps pounding as Freed ran for the street below.

"Joe! The fire escape!" yelled Frank, pointing to the top of the ladder that faced the street. The brothers started down the slippery metal rungs two at a time, watching the street below for Freed to appear.

Frank was in front, and just as he reached the second story Freed came barreling out through the ground floor door. He took off at full speed, right for the spot where the crew was busy setting up the next shot. Frank catapulted over the side and dropped to the sidewalk, Joe right behind him.

Frank pointed, and the two brothers dashed after Freed, who was tearing straight through the astonished production crew. He elbowed one man out of his way and sent a script girl head-on into a pile of canvas chairs as he forced his escape route through the technicians.

Frank and Joe were faced with a mob of sightseers and film people milling around and making it impossible to run full speed. Helpless and frustrated, they tried to keep Freed in view as they struggled through the crowd. By the time they had escaped the worst of the confusion, Freed was nowhere to be seen. The man had succeeded in vanishing again.

"Which way could he have gone?" Joe demanded urgently. Frank only shrugged, realizing that every second the thug was getting farther away.

"We *had* him and we let him get away!" Joe exclaimed with a look of disgust on his face. "What a great pair of detectives we are!"

"Take it easy," said Frank, putting a hand on his brother's shoulder. "He can't be too far away. Maybe somebody saw him."

"Hey, fellas," came a voice from under a cowboy hat. Alvin was in his usual position, sitting in his chair, tilted back against a nearby trailer.

"Alvin!" exclaimed Frank. "You didn't happen to see—"

Alvin pointed with his thumb, indicating a right turn at the next corner. "A man oughtn't to race around like that. It's not healthy, and you can knock folks over when you aren't careful." Alvin carefully adjusted the tilt of his hat. "You know, I'm beginning to take a strong dislike to Sam Freed."

"Thanks, Alvin, we owe you one," said Joe as the brothers resumed their pursuit.

They rounded the corner and entered a side street, but Freed was nowhere to be seen.

"Let's split up and check these doorways and alleys," said Joe.

The two ran to opposite sides of the street and slowly checked each possible hiding place for Freed. Then, halfway down the block, Frank saw an old pickup truck sitting at the far end of the narrow alley with its motor running. There was someone in the driver's seat, but it was too far away to tell who.

He turned and called, "Joe! Come here for—" But before he could finish, Sam Freed sprang out of an entryway and clubbed Frank savagely across the back of the neck with both fists. Dazed and hurt, Frank dropped to his knees as Freed ran for the pickup.

Joe ran across the street and reached the mouth of the alley just as Freed leapt into the pickup. It sped off, reaching the end of the alley, and disappeared.

Joe knelt beside his brother. "Frank? You all right?"

"I think so," Frank answered, shaking his head to clear it. "Freed blindsided me and he took off in that truck. We lost him again."

Joe carefully helped Frank to his feet. "Did you see who was driving the truck?"

"No, it was too far away." Frank slapped the wall and scowled. "This is turning into a totally rotten day. We can't do anything right!"

"Hey, look at it this way. Freed tried to kill us and we're still alive. It's not over till it's over, right?" Joe snapped his fingers. "You know, that truck could've been the one that dumped Fairburn's body. It didn't have plates."

"We'd better call Dad and report in," said Frank, rubbing the back of his neck.

"What about the police?" asked Joe.

"We'll see what Dad says," Frank replied.

At a pay phone they called Fenton and told him what had happened.

After making sure that his sons were all right, Fenton asked Frank, "Could you tell if the driver was a man or a woman?"

"No, Dad," Frank said. It was pretty far away, and the angle was wrong. "Why, you think it might have been Andrea Stuart?"

"I wouldn't rule her out. Was she on the location today?"

"No. Neither was Mel Clifford. But Jim Addison was around."

"Are you sure? All day?" asked Fenton.

"Well . . ." Frank thought for a second. "Actually, he got here kind of late, and then he spent a lot of time in his dressing room."

There was a brief silence from Fenton, and then he said, "I don't think we can rule anybody out. All we know for sure is that there's more than one person in on this murder, and that this guy Freed is harder to pin down than we figured."

"Don't rub it in," groaned Frank.

As Frank and Joe walked back to the filming location, Hector Ellerby came up to them.

"Where have you two been? We need you guys. We still have a lot to get done today. Have you seen Freed, by the way?"

Frank said, "Well—"

Ellerby looked at his watch and interrupted. "You can tell me all about it later. Right now we're trying to shoot some close-ups, and we could use you to keep the civilians from pestering Preston Lawrence for autographs."

Ellerby trotted away. Frank grinned at Joe.

"Just as well that he can't wait around for an answer. It saves us the trouble of cooking one up."

As they resumed work, Trish came by and gave Joe a look of concern.

"Are you okay? I saw you and Frank running after Sam Freed a while ago."

Joe grinned at her. "We're fine, but I appreciate your asking. The TV business is turning out to be more exciting than I expected. But don't worry, Frank and I can look out for ourselves."

Her look remained worried. "Well, okay, if you say so. But you just be careful. Oh, by the way, one of my favorite old movies is playing in town tonight. *Casablanca*, with Humphrey Bogart. Do you want to go?"

Joe's eyes lit up. "Sure, that sounds great! I could pick you up at—"

"I tell you what," she interrupted as Frank walked up to them, "maybe Frank and his girlfriend would like to come along. Frank, what do you think? Want to see a classic movie tonight?"

Frank looked at Joe, and then back at Trish. "Uh—sure, I guess so, it sounds like fun. I'll call Callie when we finish shooting today."

"Fantastic!" Trish exclaimed, and ran off happily.

Frank gave his brother a grin. "Sounds like you're making progress. Hang in there."

Joe shrugged. "Maybe, but I think that if she had a choice between seeing me or a movie, I'd finish a distant second."

Frank clapped Joe on the shoulder. "Well, that's show biz."

Later that afternoon, as the sun dropped low in the sky, Jerry Morrall squinted at the shot he was setting up.

"Ivan," he called out to the director. "We're losing the light. I think we'll have to wrap after this one."

"Okay, Jerry," the director answered. "We got all the important stuff we needed. If we still want a few little covering bits, we can get them with a second unit, without actors, next week."

The shot was completed, and Hector Ellerby picked up his bullhorn. "That's a wrap, people. Good work today. Let's pack it up."

Technicians began putting lighting instruments away, carefully winding coils of cable and packing up reflectors.

Frank came up to Joe and said, "I just called Callie, and she and I will meet you tonight at the theater. You ready to take off?"

"I'm going to hang around while Trish finishes up here," replied Joe. "Headcase said that he'd give us a ride back to the hotel. We're going to get something to eat before the movie."

"All right," Frank said. "Don't let her talk about movies and TV. Maybe she'll notice she's having a date."

"I'll give it my best shot," Joe assured him. Frank left, driving the rental car they'd picked up.

Joe helped Trish as she passed out the next day's schedule to everyone on the crew. Then he ran a couple of errands for Hector Ellerby. By the time they had finished, it was almost dark.

Headcase called out to them, "You guys ready to go?"

At the same moment another voice called out, "Trish! Phone call for you, in the office."

She called back to Headcase, "I'll just take this call, and then we can all leave."

The company had rented a storefront to serve as a temporary office for the day. It was just around the corner from where they had been shooting. Joe walked Trish over there and waited while she picked up the phone.

"Hello?" she said. And again, *"Hello?* Anybody there?" She gave Joe a puzzled look.

"Whoever it was must've hung up."

"Well, let's go. Headcase is waiting," Joe said, opening the office door.

They walked in silence toward the corner. Joe heard a car door slam in the darkness. He ignored it, trying to figure how to get Trish to open up a little. Footsteps approached behind them. Headcase got tired of waiting, Joe thought, and turned to say hello.

But he didn't get all the way around. Something hard and heavy came down on the back of his head with crushing force. Joe felt a flash of pain. Then the ground rose up to meet him, and everything went black.

Chapter

13

"JOE! HEY, JOE!" Can you hear me, man?"

The voice was familiar, but so far away.

Joe slowly opened his eyes, and was aware of a nasty pain in the back of his head and a blurry face staring down at him. Gradually it came into focus. Headcase was kneeling over him with his customary headphones in place and a worried look behind his wire-rimmed glasses. Joe wondered what was going on. He couldn't quite remember.

Then Joe noticed that he was lying on his back in the street. He raised himself on one elbow and winced as his head started to throb. Things began to come back to him. He looked around at the dark street and tried to focus his thoughts.

There was nobody else in sight. There was

no sign of Trish. *Trish!* He had been with Trish, and then someone had bashed him.

"What—" Joe started to say, then stopped. "Headcase, have you seen Trish? How long have I been out like this?"

With enormous effort Joe tried to get up. Headcase gently put a hand on his shoulder.

"Don't move yet," warned Headcase. "You could have, you know, a concussion or something. Someone really gave you a shot, huh? I haven't seen Trish. You both walked over to the office maybe ten minutes ago. When you didn't come back, I went to look for you, and found you out cold. She wasn't around."

Joe closed his eyes and took a deep breath.

"Can you help me up?" he asked Headcase. When the soundman still hesitated, he added, "It's all right, really. Whoever knocked me out just wanted me to go to sleep for a few minutes, not do permanent damage."

With Headcase's help, Joe stood and held on to his arm a minute until the dizziness passed.

"Listen," he said, "we have to check to see if anyone saw Trish leave and if she was with anyone."

As they started back around the corner, Joe stopped and gave the soundman a serious look.

"Be careful not to give the impression that there's anything seriously wrong. We're just curious, okay?"

Only a few technicians still remained on location, and they hadn't seen her. Joe spotted Alvin, still in his chair.

"Alvin!" He approached the big driver. "Listen, did you see Trish around in the last few minutes?"

Alvin looked up from his chair. "Trish? Yeah, I saw her drive off in someone's pickup just a little bit ago. Don't know whose truck."

A pickup truck! Joe suddenly was hit by a terrible thought. Could it be the same pickup truck? Could Trish have set him up? Could she be a part of the murder?

Joe leaned closer to Alvin. "Did you happen to see who was with her?"

Alvin scratched his head and thought. "Nope, sorry. I figured it must have been a couple of guys from the crew, you know, giving her a ride back to the hotel." He looked at Joe more intently. "Something wrong?"

"No, it's no big deal," Joe said quickly. "I was just looking for her, that's all." Alvin looked up at Headcase, but the soundman simply returned the look without giving anything away. But as they walked away from Alvin, Joe sensed the driver staring after them.

Headcase took off his headset. Joe had never seen him without it. He looked very different.

"Listen," said Headcase quietly. "You don't have to tell me anything if you don't want to. I figure you and your brother are into something pretty heavy."

Joe shot him a suspicious frown. "You haven't been—you know, listening in when Frank and I . . ."

Headcase shook his head and assured Joe. "No, no, I haven't been listening in on you or anything like that. But it doesn't take a genius to figure that something screwy is going on around here, all this bad action between you and Sam Freed, and now you get knocked out cold, and Trish disappears. All I want to say is, if I can do anything, just let me know."

Joe smiled gratefully and said, "Thanks, Headcase. I appreciate it. We might just take you up on it." He went back to the office and used the phone to call home. His father answered almost at once, almost before the phone had had a chance to ring.

"Hi, Dad, I—"

"Joe," his father cut in, sounding worried, "where are you?"

"At the location. I've been—"

"Are you all right?"

"Yeah, but—"

"You better hurry home. I have something to show you," Fenton said urgently.

At Joe's request, Headcase dropped him off at the Hardy house, and he walked in to find not only Fenton, but Frank and Callie, too, waiting for him with grim faces.

"Where's Trish?" asked Frank.

Joe filled them in on the attack he had suffered, and on Trish's disappearance.

"I asked everyone who was still around, but nobody had seen where she went, or who took her."

Fenton pointed to a piece of paper lying on a table. "Read that, but be careful not to touch it. There probably aren't any fingerprints, but you never know."

Joe bent over the piece of paper, on which a message had been pasted in cut-out newspaper letters: "We have Trish. Wait for our call. Tell no one or she's history."

Joe banged a fist on the desk. "When did you get this?" he asked his father.

"Fifteen mintues ago. We got a phone call, and an obviously disguised voice told us to look in our mailbox. There it was."

Callie spoke up. "What do they want with Trish?"

Frank put an arm around her shoulders. "Probably, they *don't* want her specifically, except as a way of putting pressure on us. But there's no point in guessing. We just have to wait for their call—whoever 'they' are."

"Do you figure that anybody on the crew knows what's wrong?" Frank asked Joe.

"Well, they know that Sam Freed is a goon of some kind," replied Joe, "but I haven't heard anybody putting things together yet. Except for Headcase. He knows that something's up, but he doesn't know what, exactly. He also said that if there was anything he could do to help to call him."

The next half hour dragged by slowly. They all sat, staring at the phones in Fenton's office as if that would make the call come sooner.

When it did ring, Callie jumped a little. Fenton picked it up instantly and switched on the speakerphone so that everyone could hear both sides of the conversation.

"Is this Mr. Hardy?" The voice sounded high, squeaky, and metallic. Someone was making sure that he or she wouldn't be recognized.

"Yes, this is Fenton Hardy."

"The girl is fine. Play ball with us, and she stays that way. We don't want anyone hurt."

"What *do* you want?" Fenton asked.

"Get Jim Addison over to your place, now. Tell him to come alone. You have one hour. When we call again, he better be there. And there better be no cops."

There was a click and then dead silence.

"Addison!" Joe exclaimed. "What's going on here?"

Fenton punched out the number of the hotel where the actor was staying. "For the moment they have the upper hand, so let's just do what they say."

The detective got the actor on the line.

"Jim? Fenton Hardy here."

"Yes, Fenton, what's up?"

"Something important has come up. I can't talk about it on the phone. We need you over here right away, and alone."

Jim Addison didn't hesitate. "I'm on my way."

When the doorbell rang a short time later, Frank answered it to find Jim Addison—and Andrea Stuart.

"What's *she* doing here?" Joe was furious. "Hasn't she caused enough trouble?"

Ms. Stuart held up a hand. "Wait, please. I've learned my lesson, Joe," she said. "I won't make any more waves from here on in, I promise. But Jim is not only my client, he's a dear friend. I want to stand by him."

Fenton said, "Andrea, wait in the living room for a few minutes."

Andrea started to protest but remained behind when the others went back to Fenton's office. After she was gone, Addison said, "What's going on here? Don't tell me you suspect *Andrea?* That's ridiculous!"

"She's caused a lot of trouble for us with her mouth," said Joe, "and she sounded willing to bend the law. We can't be sure of her."

"I can't believe—" Jim started to say.

Fenton cut him off. "Jim, you have to let us do our job. Joe's right. She's still under suspicion." He quickly outlined the situation to Addison.

"How long till they call back?" the actor asked.

"About half an hour," Joe said.

While they waited for the phone call, the Hardys ran over their list of possible suspects for Jim's benefit. The people who could have wanted Fairburn dead included Mel Clifford and Jerry Morrall. Andrea was also on the list because of her attitude. "And that's just what we know now," Fenton said. "Fairburn made a lot of enemies. There may be—"

The phone rang and Fenton grabbed it.

"Yes?"

"Hardy? Is Addison there?"

Addison spoke up. "I'm here, whoever you are. What do you want?"

The voice chuckled. "You'll know soon enough. Now, listen real close because I'm not going to stay on this line long enough to be traced, you understand."

"Go ahead," said Fenton.

"We want to make a trade. Addison for Trish. We figure that the TV company needs Addison to get this show finished, and they'll pay plenty to get him back in one piece, and you want to get the girl. Now here's what—"

"Forget it," cut in Fenton sharply. "We can't be a party to—"

"Then say goodbye to that cutie you're so worried about," the voice said roughly.

Chapter

14

"I'LL DO IT, FENTON. I owe it to all of you," Jim said quickly so the voice wouldn't cut off.

"Now, that's real smart. Like I said, if everyone plays it straight, no one gets hurt. We just want to make a little money, is all. Put Joe on the phone." Fenton handed the receiver to his son.

"Here's the deal," the caller continued. "Addison and you will drive out to Black Creek Road—you know it?"

"I know it," said Joe, his emotions on a tight rein.

"Smart kid. You leave the highway and go two miles up Black Creek Road. There you'll find a dirt turnoff that goes up into the hills. Take it exactly half a mile, park in the clearing there, and just wait. You got that?"

"Got it," Joe answered. "What then?"

"Just wait. And nobody else shows up, especially no cops. Or you won't see the girl again. We'll be watching when you arrive. If you're not alone, you won't see us, or her. Ever. You have forty-five minutes."

The line went dead with a click.

Joe relayed the plan to the group. Fenton Hardy shook his head. "It's too dangerous, Jim. You're going in blind."

Addison smiled. "It's funny. All these years of playing villains, I've been wanting to play a hero, without getting my shot. Now I have a chance to do it in real life, and I'm *going* to do it. Get Andrea in here."

When the manager came into the office, Addison told her what was happening and why.

Stuart laid a hand on his arm. "Jim, that's crazy. You'll be—"

The actor stopped her. "One reason I'm doing this is that I feel a responsibility for what's happened. I want you to stay with Fenton until I get back, is that clear?"

Andrea nodded and sank unhappily into a chair.

Addison looked squarely at Fenton. "I want to go. That is, if you're willing to let Joe come with me."

Joe spoke up. "I don't see what choice we have. Like you said, Dad, they have the upper hand; they're calling the shots for now. And if what they want is money, then they probably won't let anyone get hurt.''

Fenton frowned. Then he nodded reluctantly. "All right, Joe, we'll wait to hear that Trish is safe. But if we don't hear anything in an hour and a half, we'll notify the police.''

Jim Addison jumped up, eager to be on the way. He grinned at his manager.

"Cheer up, Andrea, I'll be fine. Look, it's just like TV. The good guys always win in the end.''

Frank spoke quietly to Callie, "Yeah, except that on TV everyone follows a script. *This* script is being written as we go along, and I wish I could be sure that we're going to have a happy ending.''

They borrowed Andrea Stuart's sporty little car. Joe drove, and Jim Addison sat in the other bucket seat. They headed out to the hills behind Bayport.

Addison was stiff and tense. Joe told the actor, "Look, I've been through this kind of thing. These guys don't play by rules. Stay loose and be ready for anything, but no heroics. They don't shoot blanks.''

By the time they reached Black Creek Road, there was no traffic. It was a two-lane strip of asphalt winding through scrubby woodland.

As instructed, they drove two miles along the dark, silent street until they got to the turnoff. This took them onto a narrow lane of graded earth, just wide enough for the car to avoid the trees that hemmed them in on either side. The lane climbed steeply.

Joe watched the numbers click off on the mileage indicator as he drove slowly and carefully over the rutted, bumpy surface.

"That's a half mile," he said. There the lane widened into a clear space in the middle of the dense forest. There was no sign of another human being. They sat listening for any hint of movement. By the moonlight Joe could see Jim's face, pale and frightened.

A voice came from out of the trees right behind the car.

"Addison? That you?"

"I'm here, and so is Joe Hardy," the actor replied steadily. "Now what?"

"Get out of the car slowly, both of you. Turn around and put your hands up on the roof."

They obeyed the orders.

A pair of hands frisked Addison and tied his arms roughly behind him. He was blindfolded. Joe tried looking around, but the voice said, "Look straight ahead of you, kid. No peeking, now."

Then Joe was searched and tied. As the ropes were being tightly knotted he asked, "Where's Trish? You said—"

He was grabbed by the shoulder and turned around. Sam Freed gave him a gloating smile and growled, "I guess we kind of told you a fib, kid. Sorry about that. But I've been looking forward to seeing you again.''

A large fist drove into Joe's stomach. He sank to his knees, trying to get his wind back.

Above him he heard Freed's voice again. ''Women are nothing but trouble, punk. See what happens to you when you fall for a dame?''

Joe was hauled to his feet, and a blindfold was wrapped over his eyes. He and Addison were marched through the clearing. Joe felt a gun barrel poking into his back. He realized that there was at least one other person with Freed. Who could it be? Certainly not Andrea Stuart. ''Let's get out of here,'' Freed growled.

Joe heard the tailgate of a truck being let down, and then he and Addison were roughly thrown into the truck bed. Both cab doors opened and closed. The truck lurched into motion and started back down the hill.

At the Hardy home, Frank, Callie, Fenton, and Andrea Stuart waited for Joe's call. A full ninety minutes passed without a ring.

Finally Frank couldn't take it any longer and said, ''They've been gone too long.''

Fenton said, ''Something's wrong. I'm afraid they've changed the rules of the game on us.''

''Is Jim—are they in danger, do you think?'' asked Andrea.

''All we know for sure is that the crooks

haven't kept their part of the bargain," Frank pointed out. "We don't know why—yet."

"No choice now but to go to the police and tell them everything," Fenton said gloomily. "Chief Collig won't like it that we've been holding out on him. But we have no alternative."

"Do we have to involve the police?" asked Andrea Stuart. "Couldn't that be dangerous?"

"The situation's already dangerous," Frank said. "They probably have Jim and Joe as well as Trish." He stopped for a minute, thinking, and turned to his father.

"Dad, listen. There's no point in all of us going to the police. Why don't you and Andrea go, and meanwhile I'll scout their meeting place. Maybe Joe left some clue as to what happened out there."

"I'll come with you," said Callie.

Frank frowned at her. "I don't know if that's such a hot idea. Maybe you should wait here just in case we do get a phone call."

"We'll go together," said Callie firmly. "It'll be better if two of us search the area."

Frank sighed, but he also knew that Callie could handle herself well in a crisis. "Okay, we'll go."

"Watch yourselves," warned Fenton, "and if you find anything, let us know right away, at police headquarters. Don't go off on your own."

"Okay, Dad," Frank assured him.

After Fenton and Andrea Stuart left, Frank and Callie were almost out the door, when Frank suddenly stopped.

"Frank?" asked Callie. "What is it?"

He didn't answer.

"Frank?" repeated Callie, louder.

"Huh?" Frank looked at Callie with a smile on his face. "Oh, sorry about that, I was just— Listen, we're going to have to wait a few minutes before we go. I've got to make a call."

"A call?" Callie was puzzled, then suspicious. "But we don't have any time."

"No, no, trust me. We're just going to look around, like we told Dad, but I want to arrange a little backup, just in case someone has plans for us, too. It won't take long. Call it insurance."

Frank was on the phone for five minutes, and then, before heading out to Black Creek Road, he stopped off at Bayport Studios.

"Wait here," Frank told Callie, "I'll just be a minute."

"What are you—" Callie started to ask, but Frank had already dashed into a building. He emerged a few minutes later and got back in the car.

As they drove off, Callie gave Frank a long look. "I don't suppose you'd be willing to tell me what that was all about?"

Frank replied, "It's better that you don't

know. Honest. Can you just take my word on that for now?''

Callie shrugged. "I guess I'll have to."

He drove along the same route that Joe and Addison had taken earlier. Climbing through the wooded hills, they neared the clearing and saw Andrea's sports car.

"They're all right!" Callie said happily. "They must still be waiting."

Frank had to drive directly behind the other car before they saw it was empty.

"It's what I was afraid of," Frank said quietly. "They've got Jim and Joe now, too. Let's take a look around for starters."

They got out of the car. It was very quiet. Frank carried a powerful flashlight and shined the beam at the sports car. A rustling noise nearby made them both freeze.

They stood motionless and heard nothing further. Frank relaxed. "Must have been an animal that we spooked," he said, and aimed the flashlight at the car again.

Just then a voice came out of the darkness, chuckling. "Just like we figured. Grab one brother as bait, and the other is bound to come sniffing around after him."

Frank flashed the light toward the voice.

A gunshot roared and Frank heard a bullet whistle through the leaves just over his head.

"Turn that thing off, kid," the voice ordered.

"All you're doing is making yourself an easy target."

Frank flicked off the light. There was enough moonlight to recognize Sam Freed as he stepped out from behind a tree, holding a .45 automatic trained on Frank and Callie.

"And you brought another dame along, huh? Well, the more the merrier."

"Where are they?" asked Frank, feeling Callie's hand clutching his tightly.

"Relax. We'll take you to them," Freed said. "We'll use your car. Let's go."

Frank gauged the distance between himself and the thug, trying to decide if he could jump him, but Freed read his thoughts.

"Bad idea, kid," he said. "Take a look to your right. Just by the trees over there."

Frank and Callie looked where Freed was pointing. They saw another figure, too deep in shadow to be recognizable. But the revolver he was holding glinted in the moonlight.

"You try any dumb hero stunts and your girlfriend gets it before you move a step. So be nice. Don't be a wise guy like your brother."

Frank said, "Why don't you let her go? She's got nothing to do with this, and she won't talk to the police, not while you have me."

"Nothing doing, kid," Freed snapped. "She comes with us. That way, I figure you'll behave yourself and do what you're told. Now, move." Freed's eyes narrowed, and he said coldly, "This is the last time I'll ask you nice."

"Okay, okay," answered Frank quickly. To Callie he said, "We'd better just go along with what they want, for now."

Callie gave Frank a nod, and a nervous smile. Freed turned toward his shadowy helper. "Help me tie them up," he called.

Seeing Freed's attention turned away for a second, Frank sprang forward, reaching for the thug's gun. But Freed stepped back and chopped at the back of Frank's neck with his gun butt. Frank fell flat on the ground, dazed.

Freed snarled and aimed at Frank's head.

"No!" screamed Callie. *"Don't!"*

Chapter

15

FOR A LONG MOMENT Freed's automatic hovered an inch above Frank's head. Then Freed relaxed. "You take some dumb chances," he said. "The only reason you aren't dead right now is I want to be able to snuff you and your brother at the same time."

Frank and Callie were tied and blindfolded and dumped in the back of Frank's rental car. Freed got in front. Before they pulled out, Frank heard another engine start up. I'll bet gangster number two is driving a pickup with no plates, Frank thought.

After ten minutes the car stopped and Frank and Callie were hauled out and marched across some pavement. Then they were pushed farther, into a building this time. Finally their blindfolds were removed.

Frank looked around. They were in a large,

high-ceilinged, old brick building. Probably an abandoned factory, he thought. The rumbling sound they had heard was made by a heavy metal door rolling back as they entered. He could just make out heavy steel moorings to which machines had been attached. Dirty windows high in the walls allowed a little moonlight inside, and a few dangling, unshaded bulbs shed weak light.

A section of the vast room directly across from the huge door was better lit than the rest, and Freed took Frank and Callie there. As they walked, Frank noted that the windows were too high to offer any chance of escape. He couldn't spot any other doors in the gloom.

As they neared the opposite wall, Frank saw that a couple of portable electric lamps had been lit there. Huge rings set into the walls to anchor machinery had been fitted with chains, leg irons, and handcuffs. Three such setups were already occupied, by Addison, Trish, and Joe.

"Is everyone okay?" whispered Frank.

All three nodded.

"Hey! Get over here and make yourself useful!" barked Freed at his accomplice, who had been hanging back in the darkness. "Get these two chained up!"

The dim figure who had been with Freed now stepped into the brighter light.

It was Vic Ritchey, the stand-in.

Under Freed's guard, he quickly shackled Frank's and Callie's legs. But he ignored the handcuffs, leaving their arms tied with rope. He stepped back to survey the scene with a satisfied smile. Then he stepped forward to where Jim Addison sat on the ground. Bending down, Ritchey delivered a stinging slap to the actor's face.

It was clear to Joe and Frank that Addison was shaken, but the actor kept quiet. Next to Joe, Trish gasped. Callie stared at Ritchey, horrified by his maniacal glare.

Ritchey was fixed on Jim Addison. He began to speak softly.

"Eighteen years now, I've been your stand-in. Never getting a chance to act. Never allowed to have *my* own career, *my* own shot. Never getting the big money. All thanks to you. Eighteen years, and I've hated you every minute."

Frank looked from Addison's shocked face to Ritchey's. His eyes were burning with a crazy light. Carefully, quietly, he began to move his hands behind him, trying to loosen the ropes.

"Vic," Jim said at last, "I saw to it that you had a job wherever and whenever I did. I didn't hold you down, Vic. You'd never have been able to make a success as an actor, you—"

Ritchey cut Addison off with another slap. A

thin trickle of blood ran down from the corner of Jim's mouth. He said nothing more.

Frank suddenly said, "*Now* I understand!"

"Understand what, Frank?" asked Trish.

"Joe, don't you get it?" Frank went on. "Don't you see how the eyewitness swore that he had seen Jim threatening Fairburn?"

"Of course!" Joe said. He looked disgusted. "How come we didn't catch on sooner? I mean, even *we* mistook Ritchey for Addison from twenty yards away. That's why he was Jim's stand-in."

"Right," Frank agreed. "Same build, similar features . . ."

Ritchey's laugh echoed in the room.

"That's right, smart boys. It was *me* that guy saw with Fairburn. I made sure that someone was near enough to see when I picked a quarrel with Fairburn. I saw to it that he got a real good look at us before Freed took Fairburn away to finish him off."

"You ought to watch your mouth," growled Freed. "You'll run it too much someday."

But Ritchey didn't seem to hear, or care. He stooped down. Now his face was only inches away from Addison's.

"I'm getting a lot of money for this, big shot," he sneered. "But you know what? I would have done it all just for the chance to have you where I can tell you what I really think of you, where I can give you what you deserve.''

Ritchey stuck his gun in Addison's face, and for an instant Joe was certain he would shoot the actor right then. But Freed yanked Ritchey away. ''That's enough for now,'' he ordered. ''You keep popping off and you won't live to spend that money you're talking about.''

Ritchey shrank back from Freed's flat, cold stare, looking pale and nervous.

Frank's wrists felt raw and scraped, but he also felt that his knots had loosened just a fraction.

Joe turned to Freed and said, ''That answers *some* questions about this racket, but there's still the big one: who's paying Ritchey? Who's paying you? Who's running this show?''

''You'll find out soon enough, punk,'' Freed said with an ugly grin. ''Too bad you won't be around to tell anybody else.''

''I believe that I'm the one you're looking for,'' said a voice disembodied by the surrounding darkness. Footsteps echoed, coming closer. Frank strained to make out the figure just walking into the light.

''Well, what do you know!'' Joe exclaimed.

''I don't understand,'' Callie said.

Frank looked at her and said, ''Callie, meet Mr. J. F. Graham.''

Chapter

16

FOR FRANK AND JOE, the last piece of the puzzle had now fallen into place. They also knew that their time was short. Frank decided they might gain more time by getting Graham involved in a conversation. He continued to flex his wrists and work the knots loose as he talked.

"Tell me, Mr. Graham, did you live in Boston once upon a time?" asked Frank.

"And did you go by the name of Gallagher?" asked Joe, picking up the thread of his brother's idea.

Graham smiled at the Hardys. "Clever boys. I figured that you'd get to the bottom of things sooner or later—unless we stopped somehow.

"Yes, I'm the Gallagher that Fairburn wrote about. We did quite well, that old gang of mine—until we were busted."

"And Fairburn knew you?" asked Joe.

Graham nodded. "We were partners. He was greedy, always in debt. He'd get info as a reporter that I could use in planning heists. Fairburn got a cut."

"But you got caught," prompted Frank.

"Not me," Graham went on. "I gave the police the slip. I came to Bayport twenty-five years ago with the money I'd put aside. I took the name Graham and set myself up as a businessman, strictly legit. I even became a community leader.

"Then I got involved with this studio business." Graham scowled. "And I met the writer of Bayport Studio's first project, 'Thieves' Bargain.'"

"And he recognized you," said Joe.

"Yes, and I recognized him." Graham shook his head. "Fairburn was still greedy. He saw a chance for some blackmail. He showed me the new script he'd written. It was the story of the old Gallagher gang, thinly disguised, with the names changed of course.

"He said that unless he was paid well, he would see to it that the press knew who I was. I knew he'd never leave me alone. He had to be eliminated," Graham finished simply.

"How did you work it for Freed to get hired on the movie?" asked Frank.

"Nothing to it. I called an old underworld friend and asked him to find me some muscle with a union card for TV work. He gave me Freed's name. I brought him here, and he got hired because there weren't many experienced gaffers around. The rest was easy. Freed told me about Vic Ritchey's hatred for Addison. It looked like Addison would be the perfect fall guy—and easy to set up.

"When Andrea Stuart asked me to help get you jobs at the studio, she told me that you'd be helping your father investigate the murder. I knew Fairburn's past would be checked, and that you had to be stopped," Graham went on. "Norris sabotaged your van. I hoped that if you were hurt, your father would drop the case."

"Norris did that?" asked Frank in surprise. "He doesn't look like the type."

Graham laughed. "He did all our driving. He may look like a bank clerk, but he's quite good. He was my wheel man in the old days.

"However, we didn't stop you. Even that little message through your living room window didn't scare you off. I figured the time had come to take my getaway fund and run.

"But Freed and Ritchey got out of control." Graham frowned at Freed, who glared back. "You see, I don't kill except when it's necessary. I'm a businessman. But Freed and Ritchey—well, they wanted blood. Freed got Norris to help in an attempt to gas you in that trailer. Then he tried to shoot you, using Norris to drive the truck.''

Graham shook his head. "That was stupid. What was worse, they failed both times. But we *still* could have cut and run, even then.''

"Why didn't you?'' asked Frank.

"Because Freed wanted to see you two dead, and Ritchey wanted Addison. So they kidnapped this young lady,'' Graham said, pointing to Trish, "to get you three in their hands. I was totally against it, but Freed threatened to finger me to the cops if I didn't cooperate. So you see, *I'm* not to blame for your present situation. As a matter of fact, Freed would probably shoot *me* for telling you all this, except that then he wouldn't get the rest of the money I owe him.''

"So what happens now?'' asked Joe.

"Well, I'll hold off your father and the cops by using you as hostages until I can get out of here. There are countries where I can live happily, with no questions asked, as long as my money holds out. Norris is getting my emergency fund right now. He has also called the police to let them know that we have you all here and that any police interference would be *very* bad for your health, but that you will eventually all be released unharmed.''

Graham shook his head slowly. "That is what I would *like* to do, believe me. But Mr.

Freed and Mr. Ritchey have other ideas. So, you see, it's really out of my hands.''

Freed stepped past Graham, gun in hand. "Enough talk, Graham. Ritchey, you ready?''

Ritchey stepped over to Freed's side, now holding his own forty-five automatic. Both men cocked their guns.

Joe looked up at Freed. The thug was grinning, and the mouth of his automatic looked huge. This is when the cavalry should show up, he thought. But there wasn't a bugle to be heard. He looked over at his brother, and waited for the sound of the gunshot, the last sound he would ever hear.

Chapter

17

FRANK HARDY LAUGHED.

Freed glared at Frank. "You got some weird sense of humor, punk. What's so funny anyway?"

"You are, Freed," replied Frank. "You figure you're on top of the situation, right? But the truth is, Graham is playing the two of you for chumps, and you don't even know it. That's pretty funny, wouldn't you say?"

Frank laughed again. He tried to ignore the pain in his wrists. A few more minutes and he might be able to work his right hand free.

"Cut it out," snapped Freed, whose face was flushed with anger, "or your girlfriend here takes the first bullet—now."

Quickly Frank quieted down.

"Now, what are you talking about? Talk straight, and talk fast."

"I thought you knew the ropes," Frank said, shaking his head. "Graham is too smart for you, Sam. He hired you because he wanted someone he could give to the law. All this time he's been setting you up to take the rap. You'll end up with every cop in the country looking for you, and Graham will end up with a bagful of money, setting up a nice new life in another country. Wake up, Freed! You're being had!"

"Just a second—" Graham started angrily, but Freed waved him silent.

"Go ahead, kid. I want to hear all of this," the thug said, looking coldly at Graham.

Joe quickly realized that Frank was trying to turn the gang against one another. It looked like the best bet to stay alive awhile longer.

"That's right, Freed," said Joe. "Frank and I know about your record—two assault convictions, eight-month stretch after the second one. Some other arrests, but you were released because there wasn't enough proof. How do you think we found out about that?"

"How did you?" growled Freed.

"Graham told us," explained Joe. "He wanted to make sure that the cops would have someone to go after. A guy with a record like yours is perfect—you'll take the rap for everything."

Frank watched Graham, fidgeting, out of the corner of his eye. If the businessman had been holding a gun, he figured, he and Joe might be dead right now. But Graham was scared of Freed's temper and would try to talk his way out of trouble.

"Graham says that personally he'd just as soon have us live," Frank said. "That's a lot of smoke, Freed! With us gone, *you're* the only one tied to any crimes."

"Right!" said Joe. "Graham wants us dead more than you do, but you and Ritchey do his dirty work, and he walks away with clean hands."

"That's ridiculous!" said Graham sharply. "You don't believe that nonsense, do you, Freed? The boys are just trying to save their skins."

"I don't care if it's true or not," Ritchey muttered. "I just want to put a bullet into Addison, and I'll take my chances afterward."

"Wait a minute," Freed said. He turned to face Graham. "How *did* these punks know about my record? Did you tell 'em?"

"Of course not," Graham replied. "They're lying, I told you. They're stalling, can't you see? Look, Freed, get on with it. We can't hang around this place forever."

Frank and Joe saw that Freed's attention and anger were fixed on Graham. They had to keep it that way and play for time.

The heavy steel door rumbled back far enough for Norris to come in.

"Everything's set. I've picked up the money and notified the police."

"So, you looked up my record, huh?" Freed asked with a murderous look at Graham. "You wanted to put me on the spot, did you?"

Norris paled and backed away. Graham said, "Come on, Freed, use your head! Of course I checked your record, that's why I hired you! I needed a man who was tough."

Freed stayed suspicious. "I don't know, Graham. If you're setting me up for a fall . . ."

Graham backed off a step, holding up his hands and making a show of bafflement. "Freed, haven't I taken care of you up till now? Come on, do the job, and let's get out of here."

"Yeah, let's get it over with," growled Vic Ritchey.

But Freed came forward and grabbed Graham by a fistful of collar. He dragged him forward until their faces almost touched.

"What good does killing these punks do for *me?*" he demanded gruffly. "I can see where getting rid of them helps *you* out, but there's other witnesses out there who know what *I've* done. Why should I whack these people out for you?"

"Very well, Freed," Graham replied, carefully removing Freed's hand from his collar and smoothing his clothes out. "I'll pay you an additional twenty-five thousand dollars, you and Ritchey both. That ought to be—"

"Make *him* do it," shouted Frank, cutting in on Graham.

Freed stared at Frank and thought a moment. "What do you mean, kid? What's your point?"

Frank gestured with his head toward Graham. "Make him do some of the shooting. That way he'll have blood on *his* hands and you'll have something on Graham. It's only fair, right?"

Freed stared down at Frank, and then eyed Graham. Abruptly he walked over to Vic Ritchey.

"Gimme your gun," he ordered.

"But I—" Ritchey sputtered, and then stopped as Freed stared at him stonily.

"It's not fair," he whined, *"I* was—"

Freed said nothing. He held out his left hand and fixed Ritchey with a flat, unblinking stare. The stand-in handed over his gun and slouched away.

Freed walked back to Graham and held out the second automatic.

"Take it," he said.

Graham looked down at the gun and then back at Freed. Then he said, "Now, see here—"

"Take it, I said. The punk is right. It's time you did something aside from giving orders."

Freed thrust out his left hand, holding Ritchey's automatic. When Graham still wouldn't pick up the gun, the tough aimed his own weapon at the mastermind's forehead.

"I ain't fooling around here. You take that gun, Graham."

Graham took it. It was clear to Frank that Graham wasn't used to guns and didn't like them. The financier looked around and saw Norris.

"Norris," he ordered, "take this and—"

"No dice," Freed said. "Not Norris, friend. *You're* going to pull the trigger, and I'm going to watch you do it. I'm going to watch you shoot this punk here." He pointed to Frank. "Seeing as how it was his idea and all."

To the Hardys' eyes, Graham no longer looked like the dignified businessman. His face was pale and sweaty. He stared at Freed's gun and nodded, slowly running his tongue around his lips.

He walked up to Frank and reached out a shaking hand until his weapon was only inches away from Frank's head. Frank still couldn't free his hands. He willed himself not to flinch, to look straight at Graham, who wouldn't meet his eyes. The gun shook, and then steadied.

From the darkness a voice was heard. It said, "I wouldn't do that if I were you."

Chapter

18

GRAHAM LET OUT A CRY of surprise. Freed whirled around. "Who is that?" he barked. "What's going on here?"

Joe let out a breath of relief. He didn't know what was happening, but at least Freed had been distracted. He turned to give Trish a look of reassurance. "Hang in there," he said softly.

From another part of the old building another voice came out of the gloom. "Give it up. You don't have a chance."

"Who are you?" shouted Ritchey. He stared into the unlit expanse of the factory and then jumped in panic as a voice was heard from directly opposite the last one.

"We have you surrounded," it said. "Drop the guns and put your hands up."

Freed aimed at the sound of the last voice

and fired. The bullets whined as they ricocheted off the bricks of the wall.

"This is your last chance, Freed. Drop your guns right now." Shouts were coming at them from all around. "Don't be stupid," said one. "It's all over," said another.

"Mr. Graham, what's happening?" called Norris, his voice pitched high with fear.

"Shut up, Norris!" snapped Graham, scanning the room, his gun in front of him.

With one final, all-out effort, Frank yanked his right hand free of the ropes. He leaned over and whispered to Joe, "I've got my hands free."

"Freed's got the key to all this iron," Joe whispered back. Let's see if we can get him within reach." Frank nodded, keeping his hands behind him.

One of the voices spoke again. "This is your last warning," it announced. "You don't have a—"

Freed fired again, aiming toward the voice, and it was suddenly cut off. There was a shower of sparks.

"What's going on here?" snarled Freed savagely. He picked up one of the electric lamps and pointed it toward where he had just shot.

A small portable speaker stood on the floor. Next to it were the remains of an amplifier which had just taken a bullet in the transistors. Crouched alongside the amplifier with a microphone in his hands was Headcase. He wore his headphones and was carrying the shotgun mike that he used to pick up whispered conversations.

"Who *are* you?" shouted Graham.

"He's the soundman on 'Thieves' Bargain,' " Freed snarled. "They call him Headcase, and he *is* a headcase, too, walking in here like that. All right, you little freak, how *did* you get in here?"

"I sneaked in after Norris," the soundman replied. "You guys were all too busy to notice."

"How did he find us?" Joe asked his brother quietly.

"Tell you later," Frank whispered back. "For now, let's just try for that key."

Freed turned to Graham. "We're not surrounded at all. This long-haired nut sneaked around in the dark putting speakers all around and talked over them with a mike, trying to panic us." He looked at Headcase, and brought his gun up. "You stuck your nose in the wrong place for the last time, wise guy," he growled, aiming.

But at that moment another voice was heard from outside, over a loudspeaker.

"Attention inside the building. This is Lieutenant Weller of the Bayport police. We have this building surrounded. I repeat, this building is surrounded."

"Cops!" squawked Vic Ritchey. "The cops are here! Freed, what are we going to do? There's cops out there!"

"Shut up!" Freed bellowed, whirling to give the stand-in a look that instantly quieted him. "Just keep your mouth shut, or I'll shut it for you—permanently."

"Frank!" whispered Joe. "The key's on a ring sticking out of Freed's hip pocket! If we can get him closer, maybe you can fish them out."

Freed turned his attention back to Headcase—but Headcase wasn't there anymore. He had taken advantage of Freed's distraction to slip away into the darkness of the building.

Meanwhile, Lieutenant Weller's voice continued. "Attention, you inside the building. You will throw your weapons outside the door and come out after them with your hands up. You will not be harmed. You have thirty seconds."

Frank noticed that Norris was growing increasingly fearful, his eyes darting wildly around the room. He whispered to Joe, "Watch the secretary. He's beginning to crack. Maybe he'll give us the distraction we need."

Joe nodded back.

Norris scuttled over to Graham and said, "It's all over! We're caught! Let's give it up before we all get shot!"

Graham was scanning the building for possible escape routes. He gave his secretary an angry glare.

"Shut up, Norris! This is no time for panic. We're not caught yet, and we're going to get out of this. Just calm down and do as I say."

But Norris wasn't about to calm down. He backed away from his employer, his eyes wide and glassy.

"No! I haven't hurt anyone!" His voice was thin and ragged. "I just drove a truck, that's all! I'm not putting my neck on the line for you, Graham! I'm giving up, and the rest of you can do whatever you like."

Freed walked up to Norris, slapped him hard across the face, and stuck the barrel of his gun under the secretary's chin.

"Nobody is walking out of here, you follow me? Nobody is making any deals with the cops! I'll shoot you right here and now, friend, you hear me? You better believe it, 'cause I got nothing to lose. So stay put and keep your trap shut."

Freed walked away, leaving Norris frozen with fear, rubbing his face where Freed had hit him.

Ritchey, who had been standing off to the side, now confronted Graham.

"Give me my gun," he demanded.

Graham shook his head. "I'm hanging on to this for now," he said.

Ritchey moved forward and shouted, "No! I

want—'' Graham fired a single shot over Ritchey's head, making the stand-in cower back.

A gunshot cracked outside, breaking the momentary silence. It was followed by a fusilade of shots, dozens of them. In a far corner of the factory, glass shattered as windows broke.

''What are you shooting at?'' Freed yelled at Graham. ''You see what you started?''

Graham stayed where he was, but Frank and Joe knew that he was just waiting for the right time to make a run for it. Norris crouched down, clapping his hands over his ears.

Only Freed held his ground, gun raised, coiled and tense, like a wild animal that knows it is being stalked. Intent on the threat from outside, he had backed closer to the prisoners chained to the wall.

Joe looked at Frank with a question in his eyes. Frank gave a slight shake of his head. He wasn't close enough to try to take Freed, or to go for the key.

''Hold your fire! Cease fire!'' came the angry voice of Lieutenant Weller. The shooting died out. ''Attention, you inside. Come out now, with your hands up. This is your last warning.''

''No! Don't shoot!'' screamed Norris. He threw himself at Freed from behind with hysterical energy. Fear had given the mousy secretary a desperate strength.

As Freed bucked and lurched in his attempt to dislodge the man, the key ring in his pocket dropped to the floor. Keeping an eye on the struggling Freed, Frank reached out, but the keys were a foot beyond his grasp.

"Joe!" Frank whispered urgently. "Can you get them?"

Carefully Joe maneuvered his chained legs around until he got a foot on the key ring. He kicked out with both legs, and the keys sailed toward Frank, who caught them on the fly.

Quickly he freed his own legs, then slid over to get Joe loose. "I'll take Graham," said Joe. "You tackle Freed."

The brothers moved together. Frank hit Freed with a shoulder below the knees, knocking him down along with Norris, and jolting the gun loose from Freed's grasp. The thug landed on Norris and rolled free, reaching for his automatic. But Frank grabbed one of the heavy leg irons and brought it down hard on Freed's wrist. Freed howled with pain, and Frank scooped up the .45.

Meanwhile Joe came up behind Graham, who was peering out into the building, looking for the cops. Grabbing the mastermind by the shoulder, he spun him around and hit him with a hard right in the midsection. Graham doubled over, dropping his gun.

As Joe bent down to pick it up, Vic Ritchey suddenly darted forward, screaming, "Gimme that gun!" and leapt on Joe's back, knocking him forward. Joe arched his back and, grabbing

Ritchey's arm, flipped him over his shoulder. Wasting no time, he yanked the stand-in toward him by the collar, and knocked him cold with a left hook to the jaw. Then he looked back for the gun.

It was nowhere to be seen. Neither was Graham.

Frank saw that Ritchey and Norris were both out of it. He trained the gun on Freed and said, "It's all over, Sam. Clasp your hands behind your head."

Sullenly Freed did as he was told.

Now Graham appeared from the shadows. In his hand was the automatic, and the gun was pointed at Callie.

"Drop it, Frank," Graham called, "or your girlfriend gets it."

Frank hesitated for a moment.

"You heard me, Hardy!" Graham shouted. "Do it, right now, or—unh!"

From behind him Headcase sprang out and grabbed Graham's gun arm, jerking it up. The gun went off, unloading into the ceiling. Joe raced forward to help the soundman pull the gun away from Graham.

While Frank covered the gang, Joe quickly freed Addison, Callie, and Trish. All were shaken, but basically unhurt.

"Guess you can tell the cops to come in now," said Trish.

"Oh, right!" exclaimed Frank. "I almost

forgot about that." He raised his voice. "Everything is cool! Come on in."

The heavy steel door rumbled open.

In walked Alvin, the driver. There was no one else with him. He carried a bullhorn in one hand and a metal device in the other.

Freed stared in disgust at the driver.

"I *knew* it! The punks suckered us! Serves me right for getting mixed up with a bunch of wimps and losers like this!"

Trish was still confused. "Where—what happened to the police?" she demanded.

"There *were* no police, Trish," Frank said. "Just Alvin and Headcase and a little electronic simulation."

"What?" Trish asked, startled. "I don't follow—how did—?"

"Alvin, show the girl," Headcase suggested. The driver stepped forward, carrying a portable electronic panel like the unit that the special-effects man had used to detonate simulated shots by remote control earlier that day.

"You mean there was nobody else out there just now?" demanded Jim Addison. "Just Alvin and some electronic gadgets?"

Alvin nodded with a bashful smile. "Headcase and I followed you guys with all his equipment. Once Frank and his girl were dragged in here, we set the blanks into the walls, all around the building. Then I set 'em off."

Joe scowled at Frank. "This must all have

been *your* idea! It figures. Leave it to you to come up with something as scatterbrained as this.''

"Hey, it worked, didn't it?" Frank said. "Anyway, Headcase had a lot to do with the planning, too."

"But how did Headcase and Alvin know where this place was?" Joe asked. "How come they weren't spotted?"

"Let me show you," Headcase said, running over to where his amplifier and microphone still lay. "It's this gimmick I put together a while back. It's a tracker, see, with about a one-mile range." He brought back a metal object like a cigar box with an antenna and a couple of lights and dials. "It receives signals from a transmitter—show them, Frank!"

Frank unbuttoned the top few buttons of his shirt. There, taped to his chest, was a small flat gadget. A wire antenna ran out of it, the top of which was taped just below Frank's collar.

"See, we just followed Frank and Callie from about a quarter mile behind. When Norris came in here, I got inside before the door rolled shut and set up my speakers. I listened in on you all with that shotgun mike, and when it looked like shooting was going to start, I spoke up. And I wore a wireless mike," Headcase finished up, showing the little device clipped to his shirt. "That way Alvin could hear what was going on from outside!"

Callie said, "So *that's* what you stopped off at the studio for!"

Frank shrugged and smiled. "Well, I had an idea that we could use some backup. I figured that we might not be able to send for the police quickly enough if things suddenly turned violent. So Headcase and I sort of worked this thing out. It was his idea to bring in Alvin. He doesn't talk much, but in a tight spot he does come through."

"One more thing," said Trish. "How did you break the windows in this place if you only used blanks? That's a pretty neat trick."

Alvin grinned bashfully. "What it was, was rocks. I threw some rocks, and that's what broke the windows."

"And now," said Frank, "I think we'd better call the police for real and hand this bunch over."

"Chief Collig isn't going to be too pleased with us," Joe stated darkly.

"But since we're giving him all the rotten eggs in one neat basket," Frank answered, "I don't think there's much he can do."

Trish shook her head. "You could never sell this story for TV," she said. "No one would ever buy it!"

Shortly afterward, the *real* police were called, and a whole detachment of Bayport's finest came to haul away Graham and his men, with Chief Collig in the lead. As predicted, the chief wasn't very happy with the Hardys, but he was in no position to quarrel with success.

There had been a tearful reunion between Jim Addison and Andrea Stuart. As they drove off in her sports car, Joe heard her telling the actor how she was going to make Jim's real-life heroics pay off big at the box office.

Headcase and Alvin drove Trish back to the hotel. But before they left, she came up to Joe and smiled shyly at him.

"We still have a date for the movies," she reminded him. "I'm going to hold you to it."

"Whenever you say," replied Joe. "Provided that I can take you for something to eat first."

"It's a deal," she said happily.

Later that evening the Hardys and Callie sat in their living room drinking some of their aunt Gertrude's cocoa.

"That Jim Addison," said Gertrude, smiling brightly. "What a *sweet* man he is! The *idea* that anyone could think he was a murderer— honestly!"

"Oh, that reminds me, boys," said Fenton. "I have a message for you. From Hector Ellerby."

"A note of congratulations for a job well done?" asked Joe with a smile.

"Well, not exactly," replied his father. "Here's the note."

He handed Joe a slip of paper. Joe read the contents out loud.

" 'To Frank and Joe,' " he read. " 'Your work call tomorrow is six A.M. Please be on time. We've lost a few days, and we still have a show to finish!' "

Frank and Joe's next case:

Callie Shaw invites the Hardys to Runner's Harbor, a hotel in Barbados run by her cousins. But just as the brothers arrive, they're met by a horrifying host. Then things get even scarier. From trapdoors and secret passages to ghostly gunmen, the young detectives come face-to-face with the mysterious spirit world. It seems Runner's Harbor has a skeleton in every closet—and they're all out to put the brother team into an early grave . . . in *The Dead Season*, Case #35 in The Hardy Boys Casefiles™.